Dragon Keepers II

Demise of Dragon's Gate

By Bruce Goldwell

Book 2 of 4
© 2006-2022 Bruce Goldwell
All Rights Reserved

Chapter One

A Visitor in the Midst

After a good night's sleep, Merlin opened his eyes and began stretching. He sat up in his bed and looked around, eyeing everything about his room. He had been deep in one of those dreams that, when you wake up, you are glad it was just a dream. Getting up from his bed, he headed toward the kitchen and as he entered the front of the cottage, there was his mother making breakfast.

"I had a bad dream," he exclaimed!

"Oh, you did?" Anabe replied in her soft voice.

"Thank goodness it was only a dream," Merlin said, relieved. He could not imagine what he would have done if the dream had been real.

"Better get to your breakfast. You have lots to do today," Anabe said, coaxing Merlin toward the table.

Merlin sat down and began eating what seemed like the best breakfast ever. He was starting to wonder if there was some special occasion on this day that had slipped his mind as his mother only prepared breakfast like this one on the most auspicious of milestones.

Not that Merlin would complain about anything his mother prepared for him to eat. He just did not know why she had gone out of her way to prepare such a wonderful meal as she had this morning. He was trying to think of what the special circumstance was that slipped his mind.

As he was eating, he noticed bright beams of light coming through the cracks in the doorway; the light from the morning sun seemed to be much brighter than usual. It was as though the door itself was glowing from the intensity of the light that was peeking through the cracks around it.

Merlin could not resist and had to get up from the table to look outside. He had to see why the light coming into the cottage was so bright. Quickly, he walked over to the door and stretched his arm out to turn the doorknob.

Just as he began to turn the knob, he started to hear a rhythmic sound, almost like the sound of the wind when it brushes through the branches in the trees. As he opened the door, he was forced to squint his eyes hard against the glowing light of the sun, it was so intense. He tried to open his eyes and focus them so that he could see what was in front of him.

It took a few seconds, but as he began to focus and become accustomed to the light, he realized that he was lying on the ground looking up toward the sun. He had only been dreaming that he was back home with his mother and enjoying one of her wonderful homemade meals.

Merlin sat up and looked down at the shoreline below, from his perch atop the hill. He could hear the waves of the ocean rolling up onto the beach and the crashing sound as they washed against the rocky ledges of the cliffs that surrounded the cove he was currently camping in.

It was a beautiful place. The deep blue of the ocean was contrasted sharply by the lighter colors of the beach and the cliffs around them, which was then again contrasted by the dark grasses and trees that grew at the top. The area was overall very calming, and he would have liked to stay there for as long as he could have, if he had been in any other situation. But, as it was, he just could not enjoy any of the beauty around him.

Merlin, missed his mother, his father, and everyone he lived with, in the Valley of Dragons, so much that his subconscious was starting to play on these feelings by creating dreams that would take Merlin back there, even if only for a little while in his sleep.

Merlin had been in this cove now for just over a year; living in a cave, the entrance of which was only a few feet from where he was sitting on the ledge. As he began to come to his senses, he knew that Dracon would be along shortly.

Every morning Dracon would get up before sunrise and go off on his little hunting expedition to get food. When he returned to the cliffs, he was always happy and full from a successful morning of hunting.

Out of the corner of Merlin's eye, he caught a glimpse of something that appeared to flit between him and the sun fleetingly. He thought he saw a shadow of something large briefly cast upon him. As he turned to see what the strange object in the sky was, it had already disappeared behind the top of the ridge overhead.

When he turned back toward the ocean view, he could see Dracon flying toward him. He started thinking that it must have been Dracon flying around the mountain cliff, but he could not figure out how Dracon had gotten back out over the ocean so far, so fast.

This was truly starting out to be an unusual day. Merlin figured he had survived so far and whatever might come his way he would just deal with things one day, and one problem, at a time.

Dracon was now nearly descending upon him. Spreading his wings, he came to a soft landing at the entrance to the cave.

"I can see you had a good hunt today," Merlin said cheerfully, cocking his head in humor.

Dracon smiled at Merlin and blinked his eyes, seeming to agree with him. He then opened his mouth and dropped a fresh fish, which was still flopping, trying to escape its fate, at Merlin's feet.

Merlin reached down and picked up the fresh catch that Dragon had brought him and said, "Looks like I'm going to eat well today too."

Going over to a small stack of wood at the side of the cave entrance, Merlin picked up a few of the logs and placed them in a small circle of stones he had laid out to create a fireplace. After setting the wood in the fireplace, Merlin began clicking a couple of stones together - one of these stones, of course, being a piece of flint - to create the sparks to start a fire.

In no time at all, Merlin had a nice fire going. He was well on his way to having the fish cooked and ready to eat. Dracon quietly watched from the other end of the ledge along the cliff while Merlin prepared his breakfast.

Merlin turned to get his eating utensils from just inside the cave entrance when without warning he was temporarily startled by someone standing there between him and Dracon. Dracon had not even made a sound warning Merlin that someone was coming. In fact, as Merlin thought about it, no one was even coming up the path along the cliffs to get to where he and Dracon were.

The person was very large in stature and wearing rather unusual clothing. The cloth was a deep, silky black and resembled the skin of a dragon. Even the skin of the stranger was dark as ebony. But, other than that he just looked like a normal, although slightly larger than usual man. There was nothing abnormal. But, it was Dracon's reaction, or rather the lack thereof, that alerted Merlin to the fact that he was far from normal.

"No need to be alarmed," the stranger said to Merlin.

Merlin leaned over slightly to look around the person standing before him and gave Dracon a look of wonderment.

Dracon was just lying there looking back at Merlin, and he did not seem the least bit worried about this visitor.

As Merlin stood back upright, the person before him said, "My name is Keltos, I am your anamchara."

Merlin didn't know what an anamchara was and looked at Keltos rather perplexed as he asked, "What is an anamchara?" The word did not sound familiar to him at all.

"A soul friend," Keltos informed him. "I am here to help guide you along your numinous journey. Please, continue with your meal and I will tell you more," he said as he pointed toward Merlin's fish cooking over the fire.

Merlin turned and removed the fish from the fire, placing it on a wooden plate, which he had fashioned from a piece of wood he had picked up from the shoreline.

Once Merlin was comfortable and had begun eating his breakfast, Keltos explained to him about his purpose in having come to coach Merlin and assist him in learning about the Draconic Tome. He informed Merlin that he would teach him how to use the Tome to learn more about the dragons and where they had come from.

Even more exciting, was the news that Keltos imparted to Merlin that he would be able to enter the

Draconic Tome to journey into its history; not only in this world but also in other worlds as well. While Merlin would be able to gain wisdom and new knowledge from these journeys, he would have to be careful who he shared these things with among others of his day.

Keltos informed Merlin that he should continue to keep his journal and write about these new expeditions and the things he would learn. It was not to be until some time in the future that these mysteries, which Merlin was to discover, would become known to humankind on Earth.

Keltos told Merlin that only a select few people upon this earth would have the opportunity to learn about the things that Merlin was about to become acquainted with; until such time when the people of this earth would be ready for such knowledge. He told Merlin that there were many powerful and intelligent beings throughout the universe but not all life forms were friendly and peaceful.

"The universe can be a very dangerous place but it is a place that has unlimited resources to offer those who would use them wisely. Before the point in time that mankind on this earth can have access to them; they will have to prove themselves worthy and show that they are able to handle the responsibilities of such abundant and powerful resources."

Merlin would soon discover the things that Keltos was speaking about. He would have access to every corner of the universe to learn, grow and gain wisdom and, in the process, would have the adventure of his life.

Chapter Two

Dragons Gate

After a morning of getting acquainted, Keltos informed Merlin that the time had come for him to open the Draconic Tome. Merlin had been keeping the Tome safe ever since it was first bestowed upon him. He had never attempted to open the great Tome, which as it turned out was a very good thing indeed.

Once being appointed as the keeper of the Tome, it was best if a person was instructed by their anamchara to open and cross over the threshold of this book. The chances were great that one would find his way to great peril if a keeper were to enter the Tome without their anamchara.

Keltos informed Merlin that they would go to another place, not far from the cove, to enter the Tome. He instructed Merlin to get the book, as they would leave immediately to go where Merlin would access its secrets.

Merlin went inside the cave to get the Tome. He emerged from the cave entrance with the book under one.

arm and his staff in the other hand. He was not going to leave anything that he owned behind.

Keltos held his arm up toward the sky. Within seconds, Paradream appeared from just over the hilltop closest to them and came swooping down, landing on the ledge. Merlin had not seen Paradream since he was first brought to the cove.

"At your service," Paradream said cheerfully, the winged horse prancing around to confirm his statement, flicking his mane with great pride.

Keltos lifted Merlin up onto Paradream, placing him just behind the stallion's neck. With ease, Keltos jumped up onto Paradream coming to a rest just behind Merlin.

"Come Dracon," Keltos called out as Paradream lifted into the air.

The four of them rose up into the blueness of the sky and disappeared over a hilltop, heading toward the East.

Flying just above the tops of the trees, Paradream glided along the countryside with Dracon following close behind. Dracon was now very proficient at flying and matched each dip and turn that Paradream took, going around hillsides and over obstacles along their way.

It seemed so quiet, soaring through the air, as Merlin had not been without the sound of the ocean now for a very long time. It reminded him of how peaceful it was back in the valley where he had built so many memories. Now, he was on the threshold of an abundance of new adventures. He wondered what it would be like one day when he could comfortably ride Dracon like he rode the stallion. He was sure that he would do it as often as he could. It felt almost like it was meant to be.

Paradream took a sharp turn to the North, around a small hill, and then spread his wings, beginning his descent. He came to a rest in a grassy area just inside a small clearing, among the trees, with Dracon landing close by. Surrounding them in all directions were the tall trees of a lush, green forest.

It was almost as peaceful as the cove that Merlin had found himself in previously but in a very different way. Instead of the quiet, rhythmic sound of the sea constantly accompanying him, there was the continuous sound of chirping insects. The sun was also different here, at least from Merlin's perspective. Instead of it constantly beating down on him, with few places for him to escape its scorching heat when outside the cave, it barely reached him and was filtered extensively by the leaves above them, allowing only small flecks of bright orange to find their way onto him.

Keltos dismounted. Merlin lifted one leg over the stallion's back and slid down Paradream's side. As soon as the two of them were clear of the stallion, Paradream ascended back up into the air and then flew away over the treetops.

Pointing to a small stump in the clearing, Keltos said, "Merlin, bring the Tome over here."

Merlin went to the stump and set the Tome down on top of it. He then stood fast, waiting for his next instructions from Keltos.

Keltos drew a deep breath into his lungs then let it out slowly. He looked up toward the sky, taking in the peacefulness of the surroundings. Then he turned and looked at Merlin intently, and in a very somber voice said; "You are about to embark upon a journey that few have ever had the opportunity to take."

Merlin looked at Keltos soberly and took a deep breath. He was filled with all kinds of feelings about what was about to take place. He was feeling anxious and excited, all at the same time.

The two of them stared at each other for what seemed like long minutes but were really only a few seconds.

"I am going to take you to a world where the Dragon Lord lives. In time, we will take more journeys into the Tome."

Keltos raised his hand, directing Merlin toward the book.

Merlin took a step toward the Tome. He reached out toward it with one hand while holding his staff in the other. He attempted to open the clasp that held the Tome closed. It would not unlatch. He looked at Keltos wondering what he was doing wrong.

"First, close your eyes and imagine that it is unlocking. See the clasp unlatched in your mind," Keltos instructed Merlin.

Merlin closed his eyes and did as Keltos instructed him to do. He then opened his eyes and again attempted to unhook the latch. This time the clasp that held the Tome closed came unlocked.

"The secret to many mysteries, and that of experiencing the reality of one's dreams, lies in the ability of one to see these things already in existence in their mind," Keltos said.

Slowly but surely, Merlin put his fingers on the cover and started to open the Tome. As with the clasp that locked the book, the Tome did not open. Merlin closed his eyes and imagined seeing the book opening, and the things within it being revealed to him. He then opened his eyes and again attempted to open the Tome. As with the lock, it too opened.

As Merlin cautiously opened the book, a huge shaft of light burst out from within its pages, and the air around Merlin seemed to draw inward, toward the Tome; pulling everything alongside him in its direction. Merlin tried to stand upright but could not resist being drawn into the book.

Within seconds, Merlin, Keltos, and Dracon were pulled into the pages of the Tome and the book slammed shut. Not a sound could be heard. It was peaceful and silent, not even the creatures of the first that had continuously been making small sounds before, dared to break the silence.

As soon as Merlin entered the Tome along with Keltos and Dracon, others living within the history of its pages took note of this occurrence. Somewhere, far off in the universe, an evil and sinister being was aware of the incident. An event of such magnitude as one accessing the Draconic Tome would never go without being detected by those in the universe who would wish to use it to further their evil plans.

In deep caves, below the surface of an unknown world, sat a hideous creature, on a roughly hewn, stone throne. Although the creature was vaguely humanoid, it was a sickly yellow color, and its skin seemed to be covered in bumps and ridges, similar to that of a toad. It also secreted a slimy substance, and when he opened his mouth to speak, he revealed perfectly pointed yellow teeth, and a foul odor was released into the air.

Surrounded by a concourse of evil followers, the troll overlord commanded a select few of his followers to keep their eyes on these matters and to report back as to their findings.

In a flash, those he instructed to do so left his confines, taking a few others with them to assist in their charge to gather information for their leader.

When Merlin, Keltos, and Dracon appeared, they were standing near a circular stone structure. There were stone pillars arranged around the circle with stone caps setting upon the pillars, connecting them all together. Some of the stones had fallen from the pillars while others remained intact. There was not a sound of anything around them, not the wind, not any animal, absolutely nothing. It was as though time was standing still.

"This is the place where dragons first came to the Earth. This structure was built here, as a gate whereby dragons could come to this earth and leave at will."

The two of them walked into the center of the structure. As Merlin stepped upon the stones that were arranged on the ground below his feet, Keltos continued.

"This place is called Dragons Gate. In your world, it is known as Stonehenge. These stones will remain here for many years to come. For the purpose for which it was originally built, it will not be used again."

As Merlin turned to look in every direction, the stones seemed to come alive. Those that had fallen to the ground lifted back to their original place upon the pillars. The clouds in the sky began to move quickly overhead, from one horizon to the other. The sun moved swiftly across the sky setting in the West. Within only a few moments day turned into night.

As darkness fell upon Merlin, Keltos, and Dracon the sounds of people could be heard all around them.

They were no longer in a large open field that could be found around Stonehenge but were instead in the center of a large city, the likes of which Merlin had never seen before in his short existence. But, his eyes were drawn from the city almost immediately, and instead led to the living creatures around them.

The whole place began to be filled with life. Suddenly dragons appeared all around. There were more dragons than Merlin had ever seen. Not only did the dragons appear, but also people dressed in a manner neither Merlin nor any other man or woman on this world had ever seen.

There were beautiful maidens dressed with gemstones fashioned like clothing, that hung from their waist as ornaments and a sheer cloth that hung down just below their knees, covering them. Their skin was bare from the waist up except that their breasts were covered by a cloth that wrapped all the way around them, just under their arms. All of them had long, beautiful hair; some so long it nearly touched the ground.

The men were very muscular and wore a cloth that draped over one shoulder, and wrapped around their waist, stretching down to just below their knees. Their shoes were strapped, leather bindings with soles. Both men and women wore beaded necklaces with gemstones that varied in design and color.

"The women you see are dragon maidens, and the men are pages. You will find out more about them later. From this point on, we exist within the Tome, during the time when dragons used this gate to come to the Earth."

Just as Keltos spoke the words, Merlin found himself standing there in a long white robe. Around his neck was a silver necklace with a gemstone surrounded by a curling dragon. The only thing that remained with him from when he entered the Tome was his staff.

Chapter Three

World of the Dragon Lord

Dragons, dragon maidens, and pages were passing through the gate with ease. While some would appear inside the circle of stones, having come from other places, others would step into the area inside the circle of pillars and then vanish in an instant. The gate was, in fact, an open door to the universe.

As they watched dragons and the many others passing through the gate, Keltos said to Merlin, "Many years before your time, dragons, as well as others, were able to pass through this gate and come to your world and use it to go to other places in the universe. There are numerous worlds in the cosmos, each having something of beauty that drew those from other places to visit them. Earth is one of those places that the dragons and others loved to come to and play."

Merlin was wondering what could have happened that changed all of this. He also wondered who the others were that Keltos was referring to. This and so much more was about to be revealed to Merlin.

"I am going to take you to one of the worlds where dragons herald from. There you will meet the Lord of dragons and find the answers to many of the questions, I am sure you are contemplating."

As Keltos finished speaking, Merlin saw everything around him begin to vanish. It was not that those things were disappearing but rather that Merlin, along with Keltos and Dracon, was passing into the gate and being thrust through space at lightning speed.

They were traveling past stars and galaxies so fast that the lights from these systems seemed to merge together to create a beautiful stream of light, with an endless multitude of colors. The stars that Merlin used to look at in the darkness of the night sky were all quickly left behind, as the three of them traveled to a place that could not be seen by the naked eye from the world that they had just left.

Suddenly the colorful light that surrounded Merlin turned to darkness. He had stopped moving and it was as though he was caught in the very darkness of space, void of any light, sound, or tangible thing.

Within moments, all around him, things began to materialize. People, as well as dragons and other creatures, began to appear. They had reached another gateway located here on this world where Keltos had now taken Merlin and Dracon. They were appearing here, through this gate, just as Merlin had watched those appearing through the gate back on his world.

As Merlin looked about, he saw dragons and what seemed like an endless array of other creatures moving about. Unlike back in Merlin's world, in this one there existed a wide range of people as well as other creatures the likes of which Merlin had never seen.

There were what looked like horses walking about, that had one horn protruding from the center of their head, and what looked like small people with wings flying about. There were dragon maidens, like the ones Merlin had seen at the gate on Earth, along with the dragon pages. There were also other creatures, which were very fascinating to contemplate.

Dragons, as well as others, were disappearing and appearing through the gate where Merlin now found himself standing. The Dragon's Gate was truly a threshold through which life forms from galaxies all over the universe could move from one world to another.

Dracon too was enthralled by the appearance of all these creatures. Though he was still young and had not even seen much of the things that existed on Earth, all of the creatures that surrounded him now had totally captivated his attention.

"Come, follow me," Keltos instructed.

As the three of them left the gateway, Merlin began taking in all the sights and sounds of everything around him. Dracon too was turning his head from side to side trying to take it all in.

"This is a world where the Lord of dragons resides. It is peaceful here and creatures, as well as people from worlds all over the universe, come here for many reasons. Some come to learn from the knowledge masters, which include not only dragons but humans and others as well. Just as on your planet, you have people who have much wisdom and knowledge that teach those who are willing to learn, the same is true in this world and worlds all around the universe."

Merlin was amazed at the seemingly limitless kinds of creatures and people he was seeing. Though he was very happy in the valley where he had grown up, he had led somewhat of a sheltered life there. Now that he was privy to the fact that there were many more things he could learn about in the universe, he had no desire to go back to the valley even if he could. He wanted to learn everything possible about this world and any other world he might have the pleasure to visit.

As they continued walking down the street, toward the citadel where the Lord of dragons resided, Keltos continued to enlighten Merlin about some of the things he was seeing now before him.

"The creatures with the one horn are unicorns. They come from a world that is magical. Of course, any world that has something quite different from that of another world, which can inspire and captivate one's imagination, would seem magical to an outsider visiting for the first time. Nevertheless, the world where unicorns reside is magical indeed. I will take you there at another time."

Merlin began to wonder how many worlds he could potentially visit during his life. Since he had to be careful to whom he revealed these things, what was he to do with the things he would learn here and in other places he would visit?

All of this, of course, would be revealed to Merlin in time. Merlin's anamchara knew all too well that Merlin was going to receive some very welcome surprises as he led him on this mystical journey into these other worlds.

"Those little creatures you see flying about us are fairies. Some fairies are so small that you would never be able to see them with your naked eye unless they wished for it, some fairies are a little larger, almost the size of regular humans. It is important to keep in mind that most are very mischievous. However, if you have a lot of patience, you can deal with their shenanigans. For the most part, they are quite harmless and are only having fun in their own peculiar way. The fairies love being around unicorns and you will find a lot of them in the world where unicorns dwell as well as the worlds where unicorns travel to visit. Whenever and wherever you see a fairy, there is probably at least one unicorn somewhere close by. Fairies frequently visit your world."

"There are fairies in my world?" Merlin questioned Keltos, somewhat flabbergasted.

"Yes, of course!" Keltos replied to Merlin. "They love to go to your world, not just to be mischievous, but because they find the people that live there very interesting. Not to mention the fact that occasionally a unicorn or two do find their way there. There are only a few select places that fairies will visit on your earth, but because fairies can be very annoying, it is probably best if they do not inhabit every community of people there. They are very good at remaining hidden so that people do not know they are around. Only rarely can one catch a glimpse of a fairy."

This was all very enlightening to Merlin. Not only were fairies visiting his world but unicorns as well. What other kinds of creatures were visiting the Earth? Moreover, how would he know which people or creatures were truly from his world? These matters Merlin would probably learn in time and he realized he would have to have much patience. From what he could tell, the universe did look quite huge and he was sure he could not learn everything in one day. He thought it would probably take a lifetime and that most likely that would not allow anyone, including himself, enough time to take it all in.

As the three of them rounded a corner in the road, there in front of Merlin, on a hill not too far away, was the most incredible building he had ever seen. This had to be the citadel that Keltos mentioned that he was taking Merlin to visit. It was the largest of all the buildings here. It was a tall building, made up of a strange, white stone that was known as marble. The curved roofs of all the towers were made up of what appeared to be, and was, gold.

As they got closer to the citadel, the area on each side of the path on which they were walking was surrounded by water. The street turned into a bridge that led up to the castle. Merlin looked off to one side of the bridge and could see another circled pillar of stones in the middle of the lake. It appeared to be another gateway. There was another type of creature using the gate to enter or leave this world.

Merlin went to the side of the bridge and looked over the balustrade. When he looked down into the water, he could see the creatures that were swimming about near the bridge. There truly must be no end to the types of creatures that lived in the universe.

Dracon too was looking over the railing of the bridge admiring the creatures that were swimming about.

"The females are mermaids and the males are mermen," Keltos began telling Merlin. "They spend most of their time in the water as they can not survive for very long on dry land. However, occasionally, they have been known to venture onto land, when they find something that attracts their attention enough that they have to satisfy their curiosity."

"Are you going to tell me that these creatures have been to my world as well?" Merlin asked Keltos.

"Well, they have been known to go there," Keltos informed Merlin. "If there is a world in the universe that has something that will attract those of other worlds to it, eventually word gets out and creatures and people from other places will find their way there. Your world is a curiosity to many in the universe. Now that your existence and place in the cosmos will be known by your having visited the Lord of dragons, I would not be surprised to hear that eventually, you don't have a visitor or two come to see you in your world. Things do have a way of getting around in the universe."

"When we first entered the Tome and arrived at Dragons Gate, it was destroyed. How can others visit me in my world if the gate is destroyed?" Merlin asked.

"That is one of the reasons I have brought you here to meet the Lord of dragons. He is going to explain all of this to you."

They continued on their way toward the citadel where the Lord of dragons dwelled. As Merlin approached the edifice, he realized that it was much larger than what it appeared to be from a distance. This castle of the Lord of dragons seemed to be even larger than the mountains that surrounded the valley where Merlin lived. Merlin wondered what he might find when he entered the edifice.

Chapter Four

Entering the Citadel

Passing underneath the large arches at the castle entrance, Keltos led Merlin and Dracon up to the door where they would enter into the bastion. There were no guards standing at the entrance to this fortress. There was no need for such at this place. A force that could not be matched by any evil that may attempt to enter these gates protected the world of the Dragon Lord. While those that would do harm to others may find their way into other realms and worlds to do folly there, an intruder to this world could not match the power that resided here, so they dare not attempt such. All that walked upon the world of the Dragon Lord did so with the knowledge that they were safe from harm. Moreover, those that would do harm in other places should dare not attempt such foolishness whilst here on this world.

As they approached the entrance to the Dragon Lord's castle, Merlin admired the marvelous carvings in the doors and the opening surrounding them. The artisanship was superb and it made him think about his father, whose work was reminiscent of this form of art. He would have liked to have his father with him at this very moment.

As Merlin tilted his head back to look up at the doors, he was amazed at how enormous they were. He was anxious to see what was on the other side. Dracon too, admiring the immense edifice, was all too ready to enter as well.

"Close your eyes," Keltos instructed Merlin. "See the doors opening before you."

Merlin closed his eyes and did as Keltos instructed. The instant that Merlin began to see the doors opening before him he heard a rumbling sound and the ground beneath his feet began to shake. Opening his eyes Merlin watched as the huge doors began to swing inward. The ground under his feet continued to vibrate as the mammoth doors opened wide.

Once the doors stopped moving, the ground again was silent. Keltos stepped forward and entered through the massive doorway. Merlin and Dragon followed close behind. Just as the three of them cleared the opening, the two huge doors closed, grinding loudly behind them.

Merlin and Dragon began looking all about admiring the huge entryway where they were standing. It was so impressive. How can any singular building be as large as this one? They were standing in what was just a small part of this superstructure and yet it already seemed endless in size.

There were columns adorned with amazing carvings at the base and tops of each column and the ceilings too were festooned with beautiful paintings. The paintings and carvings were a beautiful mixture of scenes containing different creatures, in various different poses. Each one was captured with such immense accuracy that Merlin thought that they might come to life at any moment. It was all so awe-inspiring and yet this was just the entry of the citadel. What would the rest of this edifice hold in store for eyes to see?

As the three of them stood there in the massive front chamber of the citadel, a small accompaniment of beings could be seen walking toward them. Coming toward Merlin, Keltos and Dracon were; a dragon, dragon maiden, and page. Within moments, the welcoming host arrived at the place where Merlin was standing.

"Ah, Keltos. 'Tis good to see you again dear friend," spoke the dragon. "I see you have brought a much-welcomed guest with you as well. We have been expecting him for some time now."

Merlin was astounded to hear the dragon say they were expecting him. How could they have even known about him? He was just a boy growing up in a quiet valley in another world far away from this one.

He had to pause for a moment as he gazed at the magnificent creature in front of him. It was even larger than Merlineld had been, and had a bright blue color that he might have missed if the creature flew high in the sky on a sunny day, but that definitely did not blend into its environment now. Merlin could immediately tell that this dragon was very powerful. It just oozed strength. And he almost bowed in its presence.

"It's good to see you again too, Roz. This is Merlin. And this young dragon is Dracon," Keltos said, introducing his two guests.

"You are both welcome here. The Dragon Lord will be pleased that you have arrived and is definitely looking forward to meeting you," Roz replied.

Both Merlin and Dragon turned and looked at each other in puzzlement and wonder. After giving each other a bit of a nod, they turned their attention back to the dragon that greeted them once more.

"Let me introduce you to Aeem and Kadil. Aeem will be Dracon's maiden and Kadil his page. They will see to his needs while you are here in this world," Roz informed Merlin.

Aeem was a young maiden girl about Merlin's age, and Kadil a bit older. Aeem smiled at Merlin and curtsied. Kadil bowed his head at both Merlin and Dracon.

"You have arrived just in time for the celestial fête. The festival will be in two days and much preparation is underway for the event. We will be expecting Merlin to take part in the celebration and in the competitions that will take place. Kadil will help Dracon in preparing for the festival and Aeem will assist Merlin in his preparations," Roz said.

"I am sure Merlin and Dragon will both enjoy the fête and I will assist Aeem and Kadil in preparing Merlin and Dracon for the event," Keltos assured Roz.

"A banquet is being prepared for this evening, where Merlin will meet the Dragon Lord. In the meantime, Aeem and Kadil will show Merlin and Dracon to their quarters where they will stay while they are here."

Roz bowed his head at Merlin bidding him farewell.

Keltos looked at Merlin and said, "Go with Aeem and Kadil now. I will see you later at the banquet."

Aeem raised her hand toward Merlin, indicating that he should follow her. Aeem turned in the direction she had come from and began leading Merlin and Dracon away from the castle entry. As Merlin and Dracon passed the place where Kadil was standing, Kadil turned and followed close behind the three of them.

As Aeem disappeared with the guest she was leading away, Roz said to Keltos, "As you know, while they are here, they are in no danger. We will do all we can to prepare them for what is in store for the two of them. Once they leave this world, it will be up to you to protect them."

Keltos nodded his head in agreement. He was confident in his ability not only as Merlin's anamchara but also as one who would protect Merlin from the impending dangers that were before him.

At that very moment, a few of the troll overlord's faithful followers entered the dragon's gate where Merlin, Keltos, and Dracon had first appeared here on this world. They had disguised themselves so as not to be recognized. The disguises they wore would not draw any attention since the draconic celestial festif was so near. It was not uncommon for anyone to begin wearing costumes days before the celebration.

The spies left the gate and melded into the crowds along the street. They began their hunt to find out about the stranger who had entered the Tome and come to rest on this world.

Chapter Five

A Diplomats Quarters

Kadil opened the doors to the quarters where Merlin would be staying during his visit. As the doors swung open, Aeem led Merlin into the room then turned toward him and stretched her arms out as if to say, "Make yourself at home."

Merlin had been so overwhelmed by all the sights in the hallway outside, that he had almost not realized that those who accompanied them had stopped. What he saw inside the door was almost as amazing as what he had seen outside.

Merlin was astonished not only at the size of the accommodations but also at the lavish furnishings. Never in his wildest imagination had he ever considered such a thing. Compared to the way he had been living for the last year this place made him feel like he had just become a king.

"This is your room," Aeem said softly.

To Merlin's ears, Aeem's voice was like that of an angel. He had never heard an angel's voice before but he imagined Aeem's might be the closest voice he may ever come to hear. It might have been that, since he had been in the cove with only the company of Dracon for so long, any female's voice would sound like an angel's voice to him.

On one side of the room, Kadil pulled back the curtain revealing a rather large bedding area. It was unusually large for someone of Merlin's size. Aeem walked over to where Kadil was standing and pointing to the area beyond the curtain said, "This is where Dracon will be sleeping."

Merlin and Dragon looked at each other in amazement. This was way too much for either of them to fathom. A room that was not only for Merlin to live in but would also be the place where Dracon would stay as well. Dracon had always slept outside the cave entrance back at the cove. In all probability, both Merlin and Dracon were both going to enjoy this immensely.

Aeem indicated to Merlin to follow her. She then walked to the other side of the huge room through an archway leading into another area. Again stretching her arm out, she said to Merlin, "This is your sleeping quarters."

The room was circular in shape and contained a bed the likes of which Merlin had never seen. The circular bed had three columns, with carvings running the length of each one. At the top of the three columns was a round, decorative top, with curtains hanging from in between the columns. The bed was in the center of the room and there were elaborate murals on the walls as well as on the vaulted cathedral ceiling overhead.

Merlin went to one of the windows in the room. As he looked out the window, he was astounded by the amazing view from this height. In the waters of the lake adjacent to the castle, he could see the mermaids and mermen playing, although they seemed to be like little ants from that great distance. The sun was about to set beneath the horizon, and the vivid hues of the evening sky over the mountains in the distance were more beautiful than anything he had ever seen.

Dracon went to the window and stood next to Merlin. The two of them watched as the sun appeared to touch the top of the mountains as they began moving down over the horizon. The sky was aglow with radiant colors.

"Merlin," Aeem said, pulling him out of his awe as she pointed to a room connected to his sleeping quarters. "In here you will find a change of clothes. You can pick from any of the garments available here. The lavatory is in here as well. Kadil will see to the preparations of Dracon for this evening's festivities. I will return shortly to accompany the two of you to the dining chambers."

Merlin thanked Aeem for her kindness and watched as she exited the room. He then turned to Kadil and asked, "What is a lavatory?"

Kadil smiled and raised his hand indicating for Merlin to follow him. He led Merlin through the doorway into the room where Aeem had said Merlin would find a change of clothes and the lavatory. Dracon could not go with the two of them, as the doorway was much too small for him to enter.

As Merlin and Kadil entered the room, Merlin looked to one side where there was a small room with an assortment of clothing hanging on a rod. All his life he had only had two sets of clothes to wear. Here, hanging in this small room, was an assortment of attire that he thought would last a person a lifetime.

Kadil cleared his throat, getting Merlin's attention. As Merlin turned his head, Kadil pointed to yet another room connected to this one and said, "This is the lavatory."

Merlin looked inside the room seeing some fixtures that were quite new to him. There was what looked like the bowl that sat outside the door of his home in the valley, which apparently was a place for one to wash their hands. There was a large, basin-like fixture, large enough for a person to sit down inside it. In addition, there was a seat with an opening at the top and it only took Merlin a few seconds to figure out what that was.

"Apparently, where you come from, this is not the kind of room that you had access to," Kadil said to Merlin confirming what was obviously true.

"No. But it is apparent what these things are used for," Merlin muttered to Kadil.

Kadil walked over to the bathing tub and turned the water on for Merlin. The water began pouring into the tub. Then Kadil opened a cabinet and pulled out a towel and washcloth, handing them to Merlin.

"It won't be long until Aeem comes to escort the two of you for dinner. I am going to tend to Dracon while you prepare here. If you need anything, feel free to call me."

Kadil exited the lavatory and went to prepare Dracon for the evening's festivities.

Merlin began undressing and stepped into the large, water-filled structure to bathe. He laid his head against the raised back of the fixture, enjoying the nice, warm water, before promptly scrubbing himself until he was cleaner than he could ever remember being. If he was going to meet the Dragon Lord, then he was going to make a good first impression.

Chapter Six

A King's Banquet

Aeem knocked at the door to Merlin's quarters and within seconds, Merlin opened the door, looking rather handsome standing there in the clothing that he had selected from the closet. He had been unsure of what would be suitable for the occasion, especially given how unfamiliar he was with the clothing in this world, but he had simply chosen what seemed to be the most lavish, with the richest colors and most impractical fabric. It seemed that he had been correct in his assumptions. However, he was quite taken by the maiden standing there before him.

There, at arm's reach, Aeem stood, adorned in the most beautiful dress that Merlin had ever had the opportunity to cast his eyes upon. The jewelry she wore was so bright and beautiful, but most of all, Merlin was taken by the extreme beauty of Aeem herself. He stood there speechless.

Dracon looked at Merlin, wondering why he was standing there motionless. Of course, he was too young to understand the attraction that was taking place at that very moment between Merlin and Aeem.

"I trust the two of you are ready," Aeem said.

Merlin, mustering up the ability to speak, replied, "Yes. Yes, we are ready."

Aeem motioned with her hand for Merlin to follow, then turned and began walking down the corridor, away from Merlin's quarters. Merlin and Dragon followed close behind her. Merlin, of course, could not take his eyes off the beautiful maiden leading the way in front of him.

When the three of them reached the end of the corridor they were walking through, they turned to go down another one that was much larger. Now, in front of them, Merlin and Dragon could see other dragons, maidens, and pages entering from other corridors connected to the one they were in heading toward a huge archway at the end of the hall.

One by one, dragons, maidens, and pages all disappeared as they turned in one direction or another just as they passed through the archway. As Aeem entered through the archway, she too turned with Merlin and Dracon only steps behind her. As Merlin went through the archway following her, he finally was able to take his eyes off Aeem.

As they entered the mammoth room, there before Merlin, was an enormous dining room filled with what looked like hundreds of dragons and other creatures. The size of the room was so immense that Merlin knew for sure that the whole valley where he grew up could have fit in the edifice. Even with as many creatures as were already in this enormous structure, more continued to pour in from other archways in the walls surrounding the room.

Dragons began to split off from the maidens and pages that accompanied them to find their way to huge tables on the outer areas of this huge dining area. Merlin and Dracon continued to follow Aeem as she led them toward the center of the whole gathering.

Before they reached the center, Merlin could see Kadil just before them standing waiting for their arrival. As Merlin and Dracon got to where Kadil was standing, Kadil motioned Dracon to follow him. Kadil led Dracon to a table close to the center area, a place specifically set aside for Dracon.

Aeem continued forward, leading Merlin to a table right in the middle of the whole gathering. She pointed to a seat at the table that was reserved just for Merlin. She stood by the seat, right next to where Merlin was to sit.

When Merlin reached the place right behind his seat and stopped, the whole room went quiet.

At that moment, from one of the archways leading into the edifice, Keltos entered the room, and right behind him was Roz, the dragon that greeted Merlin and Dragon when they arrived at the castle.

Immediately behind Keltos and Roz, the largest and most magnificent dragon that Merlin had ever seen, came walking in through the entryway. There was not a sound in the whole gathering to be heard. Every creature in the huge room watched as Keltos, Roz, and the dragon following them, made their way to the center of the gathering.

Merlin knew within his heart that the dragon being led into the room could only be the Dragon Lord. He was the most enormous living thing Merlin had ever seen and he was truly a magnificent-looking creature. His scales shone with a glimmer that Merlin had never seen in that of any other dragon. And, instead of being made up of a single color, it was almost as if it was made up of a multitude, a sort of iridescence that reminded him of looking up into the night sky and seeing millions of multicolored stars in the distance.

Once the three of them got to where Merlin was, the Dragon Lord took his place at the head of the table and everyone in the edifice took their place as well.

Immediately after they were all seated, a stream of servers came, pouring from the archway leading into the edifice, with trays of food that were placed on tables all throughout the dining room. Hundreds of workers passed in and out of the archways. They seemed to come from all directions, bringing tray after tray of food. There was an unending procession of workers, whose sole job was to ensure that every table at the dinner was filled with enough food for all seated.

Once every table in the dining room had been set with food, the room again became quiet as all within the edifice waited for word to begin eating. All eyes from every being and creature were looking upon the Dragon Lord. The Dragon Lord looked about the huge room and then nodded his head, indicating to all, to partake.

The silence was broken as food began being served up from the trays in the center of the tables. Silverware could be heard clicking against bowls as people and others began dipping into the crockery to partake of the food before them.

The sounds of voices were heard all throughout the edifice as everyone began conversing with each other.

From balconies along the walls of the huge edifice, music began streaming across the room. This gathering was much like the town celebrations that Merlin attended back home in the valley, but on a much larger scale.

Here was Merlin, sitting at a table only a few feet from the Dragon Lord. The last time Merlin sat at a table for a gathering such as this, sitting at the center of the gathering was with the Wizer, the wisest of the wise on the Counsel of Wisdom. Though Merlin, in his heart, missed everyone from the valley, he knew this was the place he needed to be at this very moment. Right here! Right now!

As Merlin was eating, he heard a voice say, "Merlin, I trust your quarters suit you."

It was the voice of the Dragon Lord. Merlin quickly swallowed the portion of food that was in his mouth and replied, "Very much so."

"Very good," replied the Dragon Lord. "We all want to make your stay here as comfortable as possible. If there is anything you are in need of, please don't hesitate to let someone know."

"I will," Merlin responded.

The Dragon Lord turned to speak to Keltos, who was sitting silently at his side.

Aeem said to Merlin, "I know that you have come from a world that is far-far-away. All worlds are far from here, however, I understand that your world is a very special place."

"Well, it is special to me. I have not seen my family for quite some time now and I am concerned for their safety," Merlin said.

"You are in safe hands with Keltos. He is one of the Dragon Lord's most trusted guardians. The Dragon Lord assigned him as your anamchara because he is someone that the great Dragon Lord can trust to protect you above all others. Because he is very wise, he is well qualified to teach you the many things you will need to know. And I am sure your family is safe, Keltos will have already seen to it that their welfare is taken care of."

With those words of reassurance, Merlin seemed to relax. Any worries that might have remained with him until now were all fading as he began to appreciate the fact that everyone he loved and held dear was being watched over, even if he did not understand how that was being done, exactly.

Outside the walls of the Dragon Lord's castle, the troll overlord's spies were mingling about, trying to find out what they could about the visitor that just came to this world.

Since so many visitors come to the Dragon Lord's world, those on the streets could not possibly know to which visitor the spies were referring. For those that were not in attendance at the dinner going on in the castle, they only knew that there were many visitors to their world on this day for the occasion of the banquet going on in the castle tonight.

It seemed the troll overlord's spies had their work cut out for them. The celestial fête was to be held the day after tomorrow and there would be even more visitors coming for the celebration.

"Do you have a girlfriend where you come from?" Aeem asked Merlin.

"I have been living by myself for quite some time now. My family and I were separated when we left the valley where I was born and I have not seen them since. I have been living in a cave, near the ocean."

"It must be lonely there," Aeem said.

"I have had Dracon to keep me company. I venture out now and then to explore places around the cove but I never go too far. This is the furthest I have ever traveled."

Aeem smiled as she became aware of the fact that Merlin did not have anyone special with whom to associate.

Merlin could sense that Aeem was interested in him.

The two of them continued their conversation. For a moment, all the sounds of voices and music seemed to fade away as the two of them shared stories and learned more about each other.

Keltos looked over from where he was sitting and noticed that Aeem and Merlin were getting along very well. He could sense as well that Merlin and Aeem had taken to each other. Keltos looked at the Dragon Lord, winked at him, and indicated with a gesture of his head that the Dragon Lord should look in the direction of Merlin.

The Dragon Lord sensed what Keltos had just become aware of, that being that Merlin and Aeem were making a connection. He stood up from his place at the table and called for everyone's attention.

Within moments, there was silence in the room. All eyes turned toward the Dragon Lord.

"As you all know, we have a special guest with us tonight."

All eyes now looked toward Merlin. Merlin looked around to see everyone in the room looking in his direction.

The Dragon Lord continued. "This young man has come to us from a world far from here, known as Earth. There are many of you here today that have visited his world. I have heard much about this world from others. I hear it is a beautiful place and has many wonderful people and creatures that reside there."

"Here! Here!" Voices were heard saying in agreement.

"Merlin's world is a place where there are many who live by a code that is governed by love and trust, as well as cooperation. Just as the one that we live by in this world and the many other worlds that we hail from here today. Nevertheless, it is also a world, much like many in the universe, where some live by another code. It is a code whereby they desire to rule over others through intimidation and heartless cruelty. Because of this, his world is not always a safe place for the honest and true of heart."

The silence over the room continued. Heads shook in consternation at this truth, which was also the case in many of the planets throughout the rest of the galaxy.

"The time will come when many creatures throughout the galaxy will no longer venture to his world. The same is true for dragons. As long as we can, we will find places to be at home in Merlin's world, until the time comes that we can no longer visit there safely. In addition, when we do, it will, unfortunately, have to be in disguise so that those who would do harm cannot recognize us. Only those who are worthy will have true contact with us."

There was complete and total silence in the room.

"We have a gift for Merlin," the Dragon Lord put out his hand. "Something that Merlin can use to protect himself and those he loves. And something he can use to visit many other worlds in his time."

As everyone looked up, two fairies could be seen flying across the room with something hanging below them.

When they got to the Dragon Lord, they gently rested the object in the Dragon Lord's hand.

"Merlin, come forth!" the Dragon Lord said.

Merlin got up from his seat and walked on shaking legs up to the Dragon Lord.

"Because of the great trials and tribulations that you will have to face on your journey, on the road toward wisdom and enlightenment, it is imperative that you have something that you can use as protection. Not only that but a gift that will also open the doors of the universe to you, that you can journey to many other worlds. There, you will be taught wisdom and knowledge from those within the cosmos that will instruct you, and guide you along your way."

The Dragon Lord removed the object from the covering that surrounded it.

"I give you this as a gift to use as you see fit. Use it wisely. Never act in anger. Always remember the dragon code: strength, honor, integrity, and courage. Anyone or anything that tries to take this from you will meet a bitter end."

The Dragon Lord reached out as if to hand Merlin the object. It was a crystal sphere and inside could be seen the whole of the universe. Merlin extended his hand to receive the fascinating orb.

Placing the crystal in Merlin's hand, the Dragon King said, "I give you the Dragons' Eye!"

As the Dragon Lord placed the orb in Merlin's hand, every person and creature in the room cheered. This was truly a great honor to receive such a gift as this from the Dragon Lord.

Merlin turned and looked at Aeem. Aeem smiled at Merlin and he could tell by the look in her eyes that she was impressed by the great honor that he had just been given. She had never seen anyone that came from any world being given as much attention as Merlin. She knew that Merlin must be someone that was slated to do special work among the people of his world. She felt it a great honor to be his friend.

Merlin returned to his seat. He showed the orb to Aeem and was ever so happy to share this rewarding moment with her.

The grand banquet continued until almost midnight. Just before the clock struck twelve, the Dragon Lord got up from where he had been comfortably overseeing the proceedings and was escorted out of the great hall by Roz and Keltos. This was an indication to all those in attendance that the ceremonial event was complete.

As the people and the large diversity of other creatures began to leave the great hall, many stopped to wish Merlin well. While Merlin had been the center of attention that night, he considered it an honor to have been in the presence of all of those who had attended this gathering. No matter how much Merlin would be in the limelight; he would always retain the humility his mother taught him as a child. He never considered himself above anyone else, but rather always considered all others as equals. Any honor he received was always everyone's honor to share; as it was in the Valley of the Dragons.

Merlin and Aeem were among the last to leave the great hall. After Merlin bid the last of those in attendance farewell for the evening, Aeem escorted Merlin back to his room.

Chapter Seven

Starry, Starry Night

When Merlin, Aeem, and Dracon arrived at the door to Merlin's room, Merlin, turning to Aeem said; "I'm not really sleepy yet. I would like to look at the stars. Is there someplace we can go to do that?"

Merlin did not have to say another word. Aeem was not really sleepy either, after an evening such as this.

"I know the perfect place," she said excitedly.

"What should I do with this?" Merlin asked, holding out the orb.

"Follow me," she said.

Aeem opened the door to Merlin's room and led him to his sleeping quarters. Walking over to a nook on one side of the room, she pointed to a small stand in one of the alcoves.

Merlin went to where Aeem was standing and placed the orb on the stand. Aeem apparently had prior knowledge that Merlin was to receive the orb, and had placed the stand there before he arrived from his world.

Merlin and Aeem smiled at each other, then turned and looked at Dracon. Dracon seemed to be giving a smile in his own special way, and his eyes indicated his great joy for Merlin. However, it was late and as Dracon was always up early in the morning, he opened his mouth and gave a big yawn. Merlin could tell that Dracon was very tired, and probably would like to go to sleep for the night.

"Dracon, you can stay here. Aeem and I will be alright," Merlin told him.

Dracon blinked his eyes slowly and breathed a sigh of relief. He then turned and went to the place where he was to bed down. As Merlin and Aeem were exiting the bedroom, they turned and watched as Dracon slowly lay down for the night.

Aeem turned down the lantern that was burning to make it a bit darker in the room. Then Merlin and Aeem quietly left the quarters, to go to the place she had mentioned, to do some stargazing.

Going out a door at the back of the castle, Aeem led Merlin out through the palace gardens, and then through a maze of hedges. It was not long before they emerged from the green labyrinth. The two young people ran up a small knoll, covered with soft grass, only a short distance from the castle.

When they reached the top of the grassy knoll, Aeem sat down on the lush lawn and patted the ground with her hand, saying to Merlin, "Come. Sit here."

Merlin had never had the opportunity to spend a night stargazing with a female before this. At first, he hesitated, but then, slowly relaxing, he walked over to the place where Aeem indicated he should sit. He plopped down next to her and turned his face towards the sky.

Aeem could tell by the way that Merlin reacted that he had not spent much time with a girl. That was all right with her. She had never had a boyfriend of any sort before and she liked this handsome visitor to her planet. Secretly, inside, she was hoping that he liked her as well.

Merlin lay back on the grass so he could view the stars without getting a crick in his neck. Aeem lay back as well. Just as the two of them got comfortable, a shooting star flew by.

"Make a wish," Merlin said to Aeem.

"What?" she asked.

"Make a wish. Where I come from, when you see a shooting star, you make a wish," Merlin told her grinning.

"Alright then, I shall" she replied, closing her eyes, a slight smile on her lips.

One could only imagine what Aeem wished for at that very moment. And, at the same time, Merlin too made a wish in his heart.

As the two of them looked up at the star-filled sky, Merlin was amazed at the luminous colors of the planets and stars in the sky overhead. While the stars in the valley where he grew up were beautiful, the celestial view on this night was especially breathtaking.

Merlin began looking around, wondering in which direction his world was located. He turned his head from side to side, looking up and down, in every direction, trying to recognize any of the stars overhead.

Aeem could tell that Merlin was searching for something.

"You are looking for your world aren't you?"

"Yes. But I don't recognize any of the constellations, or even any of the stars in the sky."

"You have traveled so very far from your world that you are in a completely different galaxy. While you can not see your world from here, you can see what looks like a star, but is the galaxy where you come from."

Aeem pointed toward a group of stars in the night sky and said, "See that grouping of stars over there, with the three larger ones that form a triangle?"

Merlin looked in the direction that the girl was pointing, and could see three stars shining brighter than the other stars around them, which did indeed form a triangle.

"Yes. I see them."

"Those aren't really stars that you are looking at. They are clusters of stars, planets, and other objects grouped together to form what are called galaxies. One of them is the galaxy you come from. It is so far away that the cluster of planets and other objects in the galaxy looks like a single star from here."

Merlin, being so far from his own world and the galaxy it was part of, could understand now why he did not recognize any of the stars in the sky overhead. Looking at the bright spots in the velvet black of night, he wondered what his parents and everyone from his village were doing at that very moment. He had a feeling that there in his world, his mother was looking up at the night sky thinking about him as well. He smiled, believing that he was in her thoughts at that very moment, and hoped that soon he would be able to see her again.

Aeem could sense Merlin's feelings as he lay there, gazing up at the sky, so she asked, "Tell me about your family. What are they like?"

At that very moment, a person could not have asked a better question. When someone has been away from their family as long as Merlin had been away from his, and this being the first time in Merlin's life he had ever been separated from his kin, asking a person to talk about their home and family was the best possible remedy for the situation.

Merlin took a deep breath and the words came pouring out of his mouth. A year's worth of lonely feelings came streaming from him, and Aeem just lay there attentively, letting Merlin release all of his pent-up feelings. He told Aeem all about his mother and all the special things she did when he was growing up, and about his father and his friends, and how much all of them meant to him.

Aeem could sense with each word that Merlin spoke that his heart was overflowing with feelings of love, and a renewed connection to his mother and father who were so far away in another world in the galaxy there, in the sky above them.

Once Merlin finished sharing all the things he needed to get out at that time, he stopped talking and just laid there on the grass with a peaceful feeling, looking up at the beautiful sky overhead.

"You know. I am sure that at this very moment your mother is looking up at the sky, wherever she is, and thinking about you."

Merlin turned his head and looked Aeem in the eyes. He smiled, thinking he had probably found the best friend anyone could ever hope for. Best of all, this new friend was a girl.

After gazing into each other's eyes for a moment, they both turned their attention back toward the sky and Aeem continued to show Merlin some of the amazing sights overhead. Just like in the sky over his planet, the stars and galaxies, which were above this world, formed various shapes; people and different creatures that helped those on this world recognize various locations in the night sky.

The two of them were having so much fun that they had not paid attention to the time. It was very late now and there was much to be done the next day.

Merlin was slightly startled as he caught the shape of someone standing just at his head. As he moved his eyes up to look at the person standing there, he recognized that it was Keltos.

"The two of you are having fun I see," Keltos said.

They both nodded their heads, indicating yes, and Merlin said, "There is so much to see and learn about, I don't see how anyone can take it all in during one lifetime."

"One lifetime is all that we all have. That is why it is important that we use our time wisely, to search out those things that can help us to become all we can be. The light that you see, from the stars and galaxies overhead, have traveled millions upon millions of years, and yet the time that we live in is but a twinkling of an eye."

Merlin and Aeem looked toward one another, raising their eyebrows. There was so much that both of them had to discover. As for tonight, they both needed to get back to the castle and get some sleep.

As the two of them were getting up from their places on the ground Keltos said, "After breakfast, I will come and take the two of you to see someone very special. Be sure to get up early and have a good breakfast because there is much we have to do. Merlin, you will be in the great race at the celestial fête. The teams will be selected tomorrow. Both you and Dracon will be chosen to be on one of the teams."

Merlin looked at Aeem and gave a puzzled look as he was wondering what race Keltos was referring to. However, Aeem knew what he was talking about as she had seen these races many times, as they were held each year during the great celebration that comes at this time.

"I will see you both tomorrow."

With those words, Keltos turned and walked off into the darkness.

Aeem and Merlin headed down the grassy knoll and returned to the castle. The pretty girl escorted Merlin back to his room where the two of them said goodnight. As Merlin closed the door to his room, Aeem was heading down the hall to her quarters, smiling ever so happily to herself. On the other side of the door, Merlin too had a smile that ran from ear to ear. He walked to the canopied bed and kicked off his shoes. He did not even take the time to dress for bed. He just rolled back on the bed, closed his eyes, and dozed off.

Chapter Eight

First Day

When Dracon opened his eyes, his first thought was that of going out to hunt for food. However, just as he lifted his head from the soft bedding he had slept on that night, Kadil came walking in the door to the quarters.

"Good morning Dracon," Kadil said. "I trust you had a good night's sleep."

Dracon blinked his eyes as if to reply with a yes. Then his thoughts went right back to that of wondering where he would hunt for food.

"I bet you are ready for a good morning meal."

Kadil put a small bucket of water down close to Dracon and then dipped a cloth that was in his hand into the water. He twisted the cloth to ring out the extra water and then began to clean Dragon's face with it. Dracon had never had anyone wash his face for him. He had always been content with dipping into the waters along the ocean side and splashing about in lakes, close by where he and Merlin stayed in the cove. Having a page to take care of him was something very new to him.

"As soon as I get done here, I am going to take you to the galley where the royal chef has prepared a wonderful breakfast for you."

As Kadil washed behind Dragon's ears, Dracon twitched his head a bit, as it kind of tickled having someone rub behind them. Not that Dracon was going to complain; all this attention was just too much to ask for. He was going to enjoy every minute of it.

"There! I bet you feel a lot better now." Kadil said as he finished cleaning Dragon's colorful coat.

Kadil then pushed the bucket to one side and tossed the cloth into it. "I'll get to that later. Come, follow me."

Kadil walked over to the door of the quarters, then opened the door and waited for Dracon to follow. Dracon got up from the large bed and went to the door where Kadil stood waiting. He gave Kadil a look of gratitude and then passed through the doorway. Closing the door to the quarters, Kadil then led Dracon down the hallway toward the galley.

As with every morning that has passed the last year, Merlin was still sleeping as Dracon went off to find the first meal of the day. Only on this day, Dracon was not going to have to go very far to get his morning meal.

Turning a final corner in one of the hallways in the castle, Kadil and Dracon passed through an archway, much like the one the night before, that led into the huge dining hall. This dining room was much smaller and accommodated a smaller group of people. In fact, it appeared that Dracon was the only one dining here this morning.

"Ah, Dracon!" A jolly man with a white outfit and rather unusual-looking hat said as Dracon and Kadil entered the room. "I have been looking forward to this moment. I have prepared something quite special for you."

This jolly man was the royal chef. He had already prepared Dragon's breakfast for him. There, next to the chef, was a large bowl filled with something that looked very appetizing. Dracon was very hungry, so he was ever so ready to start tasting what the chef had made.

Pointing to the bowl, the chef said, "Benu pleazur" which was Dragon language, meaning, "for your pleasure."

Dracon went over to where the large bowl was sitting and sniffed at the food. His eyes seemed to get larger and the look on his face was one of delight. Without another word from anyone, Dracon began dining enthusiastically on the meal the royal chef had prepared.

The chef could tell, by the way, Dracon was feasting on the meal, that he was very pleased. He turned and bowed, and then headed back to the kitchen as he had others to prepare breakfast for as well.

Once again, the door to Merlin's quarters opened. This time, the small figure entering the room was Aeem, who had come to wake Merlin. There was much to be done this day and it was not a day that anyone, especially Merlin, could waste by sleeping the morning away.

Aeem pulled back the curtains, revealing the light from the morning sun which was just starting to peek over the horizon. With the light of day shining on Merlin, his eyelids opened. As his eyes began to focus, he started to recognize the figure of someone standing there beside his bed and he sat up abruptly.

"Good morning Merlin."

He recognized the voice as being that of Aeem. He shook his head trying to focus his eyes completely and could see her moving toward the adjacent room where the closet and lavatory were located.

"I will get you a change of clothes. You will need something a bit more casual for today's activities. You will be preparing for the race tomorrow, as well as being selected to be on one of the teams. I am going to take you to the galley for breakfast first, though."

She then disappeared through the entrance to the adjacent room. When she reappeared, she laid some clothes on the bed beside Merlin.

"I will return shortly to escort you to the galley."

Aeem then exited the quarters, closing the door behind her.

Merlin stretched his arms out to each side and took a deep breath as he yawned. He looked toward the window and saw the sun coming up over the horizon. He smiled, knowing that all of this was very real and was not just some wonderful dream.

He got up from the bed and went into the lavatory to take care of the first business of the day. While in the lavatory, he also washed his face and then returned to the bedroom area to put on a change of clothes.

Just as he finished dressing, a knock came at the door to the quarters.

"Yes," Merlin said as he watched the door begin to open.

"I trust you are ready." Again, it was the voice of Aeem as she poked her head in through the open door, looking around to see Merlin standing in the doorway to the sleeping area, smiling.

Merlin could tell, by the look in Aeem's eyes, that she fancied what he was wearing, and that it met with her approval.

"Come, I am going to take you to the galley for breakfast. Dracon has already been there and had his fill."

The two of them left the quarters to Merlin's room to go to the galley for a good morning's breakfast.

When Aeem and Merlin entered the galley, there, waiting for Merlin, was the royal chef, just as he had been waiting when Dracon had entered not too long before.

"Ah, Merlin!" The royal chef greeted Merlin with the same jolly voice that he had used to greet Dracon and, for that matter, the same voice that he always used, each time anyone entered his galley to eat. "I have prepared you something quite special."

Merlin and Aeem sat down at the beautiful, long, wooden table in the galley. A procession of servers came into the room, as had been done the night before at the huge dinner. Dinnerware was placed in front of the two of them as well as silverware, goblets, and napkins. A couple of other servers placed huge trays on the table before Aeem and Merlin.

Once the servers exited the room, the royal chef went to the table and took the covers from the trays.

"Benu pleazur."

With those words, the royal chef left the galley, disappearing through the doorway that led to the kitchen.

Merlin could not believe his eyes. There, on one of the trays, was an assortment of fruits and cheeses, the likes of which were fit for a king. From another tray, steam was rising up from an incredible array of food that had been cooked by the royal chef only a short time before they came in to eat.

Merlin and Aeem enjoyed a hearty breakfast together while sharing more stories about their lives. Like the night before, the time passed ever so quickly and it was not long before Keltos entered the galley, just as he had done on the grassy knoll behind the castle.

"There is much to do this day. I trust you have had plenty to eat." Keltos said, smiling as he approached the table.

As with the night before, his arrival was impeccably timed as Merlin and Aeem had just finished eating.

"Kadil has already taken Dracon to meet other young dragons, who will be in the big race tomorrow. He will be practicing the run in the leg he is to take part in. Later this day, the teams will be selected. You will go with me now to prepare for your part in the race."

Keltos then extended his arm toward the door, inviting Merlin to join him.

"I will see you later this morning," Aeem said as the two of them slid their chairs back and stood up.

That having been said, Merlin and Aeem smiled at one another for the last time that morning, then Merlin departed heading toward the door of the galley with Keltos at his side.

Chapter Nine

Training for the Race

Keltos exited the castle with Merlin in tow, and it was obvious that the whole kingdom was overflowing with life. People and all sorts of interesting creatures were all about. The castle grounds and the surrounding area were filled with everyone and everything imaginable. All were preparing for the festivities of the celestial fête.

There were those who were moving swiftly about the area, putting up decorations for the festivities. There were others who were going to be taking part in the games, and still, more who would be entertaining throughout the day. It was a spectacle the size of which Merlin thought could not be matched by any other event in the universe.

As Keltos led Merlin through the gardens behind the castle, Merlin observed the mermaids and mermen swimming through the waters next to the castle grounds. They were going back and forth, jumping out of the water and going through obstacles that were placed over the water. Merlin was sure there was a good reason why these creatures of the deep were practicing these feats of amazing grace.

In the sky overhead, dragons were flying across the sky at lightning speed and doing aerial maneuvers with amazing precision. When Merlin turned and looked back toward the castle, he could see fairies flying around the tops of the castle, then swooping down along the gardens through a myriad of obstacles that had been placed in the gardens.

Merlin did not yet understand what was going to be taking place, or how it related to this big race he was hearing about, but knew all of this activity was related somehow. In a few minutes, all of Merlin's questions would be answered, as Keltos was getting ready to reveal it to him.

When the two of them got to the rear of the gardens, rather than go into the labyrinth of hedges, Keltos turned to the left and led Merlin to an open field that was adjacent to the labyrinth's side.

There, in the open field, were dragons of all kinds. They were all stretching their wings and brushing them against the wind as if exercising them for some activity. That was. what they were doing. Merlin was about to find out what that activity was.

"Merlin, tomorrow during the festival, there will be a big race. The race is a relay, which includes creatures and people of different worlds and origins. You and Dracon are going to be given the special privilege of taking part in this race. Dracon is going to be in the relay in which the young dragons participate. You are going to enter the race as the jockey of one of these dragons. You get to choose which dragon you will ride. Later today, you will be selected to be on one of the teams that will be taking part in the race. Whichever team you are selected to join up with is the team that Dracon will be put on as well."

Merlin looked over all the dragons in the field. He was not sure how he would decide upon which dragon he should ride. It did not really matter to him if he was to win the race or not. At that very moment, Merlin was just happy that he was going to have the privilege of being a part of this amazing event.

"The relay starts with the fairies, who will fly a preset course that is laid out for them. The mermaids and mermen run the second part of the relay. Eventually, Dracon and the other young dragons will have their chance to fly in their part of the race. For the last part of the relay, you will fly with your dragon through the Mountains of Amazmond."

Keltos pointed toward a range of snow-capped mountains, far off in the distance. Merlin raised his eyebrows as it seemed almost impossible to him that a dragon could fly to those mountains in the distance in any timely manner. Merlin was about to discover that he was mistaken.

"Look around. Choose the dragon you will ride. Once you select, you are going to ride the one you have chosen through the course for a practice run. The dragons know the way. You will, of course, help the dragon in deciding when to turn and make other moves along the way. The dragons have the speed; you are the one who has the insight of what to do along the way."

Merlin was to be the first to choose which dragon he would ride, before the others who were going to be participating in the race. Not that it gave him an advantage.

The other jockeys were poised to make their selection. Once Merlin made his choice, the others would quickly make their choices and the first practice run would take place.

One last time, Merlin looked over the dragons standing there in the field. He thought for a second about his mother and remembered that her favorite color was always red. A glorious dragon, with fiery red scales, stood proudly waiting its turn. Raising his arm, Merlin pointed, indicating his choice of mount.

Immediately the other jockeys left the line in which they were standing, and one by one headed to the dragon they had chosen to ride. Keltos led Merlin over to the dragon he had selected and when Merlin stepped up near its side, the dragon leaned down, lowering its wing so that Merlin could climb upon his back. All the other dragons were doing the same for their riders.

Once everyone had mounted the dragons that they had selected, a horn blew and the dragons lifted off from the ground all at once. In the blink of an eye, they headed off toward the Mountains of Amazmond in the direction that Keltos had shown him earlier.

Merlin held tightly to the reins that were about the dragon's neck. For this first run-through of the course, all Merlin could do was hold on tight and hope he lived through the experience. Never before had Merlin seen a dragon fly as fast as the one he was on and all the dragons that surrounded him in the sky on this day. He could see the mountains fast approaching and it would only be minutes before the dragons would be upon them.

Back at the castle, Aeem watched from one of the windows in the bastion. She closed her eyes and imagined Merlin returning to the grounds from where the dragons lifted off. Although it was not probable that Merlin would reach the field first, she would be happy if he arrived back in one piece. This, the last leg of the relay race, was not something for the lighthearted. It was the most difficult part of the race and was filled with perilous obstacles to overcome.

Keltos too, watched from the field, as the dragons were about to disappear on the horizon. He had confidence that Merlin would return safe and sound. He knew, however, that Merlin would have to fly the course one more time to become better acquainted with it, and to have any chance of placing among the top finishers in the race on the morrow.

It was not but a few moments when the dragons, along with their riders, disappeared into the haze of the mountains. They would not be seen again until they appeared once more coming over the top of the mountain, just in front of the castle heading to where, on the day after, the finish line would be.

Everyone that had observed the dragons lifting from the grounds, headed off toward the front of the castle to watch for the dragons and riders to appear again on the return from the Mountains of Amazmond.

Aeem, too, went through the castle halls as fast as her feet could carry her, to get to one of the windows at the front of the palace.

When the dragons got to the Mountains of Amazmond, they all headed toward a narrow opening along the walls of the rocky ledges of one of the mountains. Merlin could see as the other dragons got to the opening, each dragon would turn to one side so they could make it through the narrow mouth of the passage.

Just before Merlin got to the opening, he leaned forward, holding his body as close to the dragon as he could. His dragon turned to the side and the two of them slipped through the opening with ease. However, Merlin could feel the rocky edge of the mountain pass just inches from his head.

Merlin knew that he had to watch closely what the other jockeys and dragons were doing as they passed through the tops of these mountains. He was taking note of every turn, and every hazard along the way. Merlin knew that it was good that he was at the back of the pack in this trial run. It gave him an opportunity to observe what the others were doing to make it through the course. He also knew, however, that he had to stay as close as possible so as not to lose sight of them.

Every now and then Merlin would, unfortunately, lose sight of those ahead of him, but the dragon knew which direction to fly and within moments, Merlin would again have his eyes on the others.

At the castle, almost everyone had gathered and all had their eyes focused on the mountain just in front of the fortress watching for the return of the dragons. Everyone knew it would not be long before the dragons would come flying low over the mountaintop and head toward where the finish line would be.

Aeem's eyes also focused on the top of the mountain, waiting for the first of the dragons to appear.

Everyone waited with bated breath, wondering at what moment the dragons and riders would appear. The sky was clear and bright, and there was not a cloud over the mountain anywhere, so the minute the racers cleared the top everyone would see them from below.

All the mermaids and mermen stopped swimming in the waters next to the castle. The fairies all found a place to rest and the people and creatures in the city had all come to a stop, knowing that the dragons would be coming over the top of the mountain soon. Almost everyone in the kingdom stopped what he or she was doing to watch the event of the moment. There was a hush throughout the entire kingdom.

Sneaking a peek from one of the windows of the castle, even the Dragon Lord took the time to stop what he was doing to go and watch for the dragons to appear.

Then without a sound in the sky overhead, the first of the dragons came, flying over the top of the mountain. As soon as the dragon passed over the mountaintop, it made a beeline straight toward where the finish line would be the next day. One by one, the other dragons appeared over the mountaintop as well. As each of them cleared the top, they each took a straight course toward the finish line.

All the dragons appeared over the mountaintop, heading straight toward the finish line, but one. The dragon

Merlin rode had not yet appeared. The first of the dragons passed the finish line and some of the others had begun crossing the line as well.

Aeem watched anxiously waiting for Merlin to appear. She watched as more of the dragons completed the course. It was looking as though all of them would finish the practice race, and Merlin had not even come over the mountaintop.

Then finally, the last dragon appeared with Merlin holding on tight. Merlin could see the line of dragons ahead of him all pointing the way to the finish line. His dragon dipped down, taking the same path as the rest of the dragons. Merlin watched as everyone below cheered as each dragon passed the finish.

As each dragon crossed the line, it would glide back up into the air to head back toward the field from where they started.

Finally, Merlin too crossed the finish line, where the breathless boy and his dragon headed toward the field as well. Within moments, Merlin would be landing in the field behind the castle.

Aeem watched as Merlin and his dragon disappeared over the top of the citadel. She then turned to head back to the window where she watched Merlin disappear into the mountains only a short time before.

When Keltos returned to the field, Merlin standing next to his dragon was stroking the dragon's side. He was talking to the dragon and commending him for having gotten him through the precarious mountains way off in the distance. Merlin was not only glad to be alive but also for having gotten back to the castle in one piece.

"Merlin, very well done. The only thing you have left to do is get over that mountain ahead of at least one of the other riders." Keltos smiled at Merlin teasing him but was in fact ever so happy Merlin had made it through the ordeal safely.

"I will do better tomorrow. I just need to go through that course one more time, then I will be ready."

"You will have the chance to do that later today. For now, your dragon needs to rest up a bit. He will want to have a nice lunch before he takes you through again. Only the next time, you will be going through without everyone else. This will be your chance to try the course on your own terms."

As Keltos finished speaking, Merlin looked up at the castle to see Aeem appear at one of the windows. She waved at him, and he, of course, waved back. He was relieved to see her, as she was to see him.

Chapter Ten

Outside the Castle Gate

Dracon was having so much fun with the other dragons that Merlin felt it best to let him remain there while he went to visit the local community in the kingdom. It surrounded the castle, and the person best suited for the job was going to show him about the kingdom, which was of course; Aeem. The Dragon Lord himself had made that decision.

When the front doors of the castle opened, Merlin and Aeem walked through the entryway just as another entourage of visitors arrived and were about to walk into the doors of the castle. As this group of people passed Merlin and Aeem, they bowed their heads to the two of them as a gesture of recognition. Merlin and Aeem returned the salutation in kind.

There was quite a bit more activity outside the castle gates than when Merlin had first arrived. The streets were filled with a lot more people and creatures almost too numerous to count. It seemed as though every creature in the universe must have come to take part in the celestial fête.

Aeem took Merlin into a few of the shops along the way to view their wares. The artisanship of the creations in these stores was much more intricate than Merlin was used to seeing. There were even items that were for sale that were not available in the world Merlin came from. At least not in the valley where he lived.

There were things called clocks, that people could observe the time of day. In addition, there were these very pretty shiny things that hung from the ceiling called chandeliers. Merlin had observed these in the castle as well but had not known what they were. There were figurines of many of the creatures that Merlin had observed on the streets. Some of the figurines were of creatures he had not even seen yet. Some of the figurines were made of wood, some were made of clay, and painted to look just like the creature it was modeled after, and yet others still were made of metals, the names of which Merlin had never heard. It was all so fascinating.

Merlin was beginning to understand why Keltos had told him that there were things he could not share with the people of his world. There were many things available here in the world of the Dragon Lord that were not yet available in his world, much less even thought of yet. There seemed to be no end to the countless number of things that those of a creative nature could imagine and produce.

Aeem took Merlin to another place, called a gallery. There were paintings hanging from the walls that had landscapes, some of the ocean shores much like the one Merlin lived at back on his earth, and others of people and creatures. Merlin knew he could spend hours going through the gallery and never get tired of looking at all the beautiful artwork it contained.

"I bet you are getting hungry," Aeem said to Merlin.

"I had just started thinking about that," Merlin replied as his stomach made a rumbling sound.

"I know the perfect place." Aeem took Merlin by the hand and started to lead him toward the front door of the gallery.

Now, this was something that Merlin had not experienced before. A girl taking him by the hand, and holding it to escort him, was certainly going to make it to the top of his list of things to remember in his lifetime. It was not something he was used to and he was not going to be disagreeable about it, much less let go of her hand.

Aeem continued to hold Merlin's hand leading him down the street to a café with tables that were located outside with people sitting at them. Finding an empty table at the outer corner, among the others, Aeem let go of Merlin's hand, pointed to one of the chairs, and said smiling brightly, "You sit there."

She then seated herself in the chair across the table from where Merlin would be sitting. As he pulled the chair back, he observed the people walking past the café, just on the other side of the railing that surrounded the tables.

"I have only eaten outside when my mom would send me my lunch in a potato sack, but never in a manner such as this."

"Hopefully this is something that you will enjoy," Aeem said with reserved optimism.

Merlin had enjoyed every moment of his visit to this world so far, and he had little doubt that this would be any different. Smiling at the pretty girl sitting across from him, Merlin knew that this was to be another one of those opportunities to experience something new and pleasurable.

A waiter came to the table where Aeem and Merlin were seated and brought them a couple of glasses of water. "Will you require a menu?" He asked them.

"Is there anything in particular you like to eat?" Aeem asked Merlin.

"I enjoy most everything," Merlin replied.

"I can order for both of us. If you like?"

Merlin had never eaten at a café before and did not know what one would do to order food, so he was very relieved and happy to allow Aeem to have the honor of doing so.

"Oh. Yes, please do."

Aeem then spoke to the waiter in a language that Merlin did not understand. When she was done, the waiter nodded his head and turned away, going inside the bistro.

As they had done at every other opportunity, Merlin and Aeem began sharing stories with each other. Merlin had lost interest in everything going on around him. He was completely focused on Aeem.

Across the way from where the two of them were seated, a couple of passersby had taken an interest in Aeem and her guest. Merlin was not paying attention to the fact that these two characters were coming straight toward where he was seated.

"Good day," one of the two said to Merlin.

Merlin, so focused on Aeem, was startled when the stranger spoke to him.

"We hear you have come from your world as a very special guest of the Dragon Lord. Is this true?"

While Merlin didn't think of himself as special, all others in the kingdom that had heard about him considered his visit quite extraordinary indeed.

"Yes. I am staying in the Dragon Lord's castle. However, I would not say that I am special by any means."

"Oh! You are quite modest indeed. Your presence is known all throughout the kingdom."

"Even the over..." the other stranger started to say something but he was elbowed by his friend and given a look that told him to keep his mouth shut.

"Will you be staying long?"

Merlin looked toward Aeem and replied, "I suppose for another day or so. I need to get back to my world soon. I have not seen my family in a very long time and I hope to find out where they are."

"Oh. I see. We hope your stay here is pleasant and short as well. Farewell for now." The stranger said as he grabbed his friend and walked away.

Merlin and Aeem did not give the strangers another thought but continued with the conversation they had been having.

The two strangers joined a small group of their associates on the other side of the street.

Speaking to one of the others in the group, the leader said, "I want you to go back to the overlord and let him know we have found the visitor. Do not stop and speak with anyone along your way back to the dragon's gate. Do you understand me?"

The one receiving the instructions nodded his head that he understood.

"Go now! Bring me word from the overlord as quickly as you can."

The individual left as instructed, and headed back to the dragon's gate to deliver the message to the troll overlord.

The rest of the troll overlord's spies all headed down the street, melding into the crowds.

Not too far from where Merlin and Aeem were sitting, another figure was standing against a wall and had observed all that had taken place. Once the group of strangers disappeared into the crowd, this other stranger began walking up the street toward the citadel.

Meanwhile, Merlin and Aeem continued to have lunch, not knowing that they were being watched over by some of the dragon lord's sentries. The troll overlord's spies themselves were unaware that their presence was known and that they were being watched as well.

Chapter Eleven

A Dragon's First Words

When Merlin and Aeem returned to the castle, one of the king's assistants was waiting for them. Just as the two of them entered the castle the assistant welcomed them back and then gave Merlin a message from the Dragon Lord.

"The King wishes to meet with you later today. He will send for you when he is ready." The assistant then bowed his head and departed.

Merlin looked at Aeem and shook his head in wonder. So many important people had never given him so much attention. His closest friends had always been his parents and he was just one of the commoners back home.

Here he was now, in another world, being treated like something special, and he had a new friend that he was starting to grow attached to. How was he ever going to leave all this behind? As always his thoughts drifted back to those things that meant the most to him.

"I wonder what Dracon is up to," he said to Aeem.

"Why don't we go see," Aeem suggested.

Exiting one of the openings to the castle, Aeem led Merlin to a small field where the young dragons that were going to participate in the big race were all playing. It didn't take Merlin but a few seconds to locate Dracon who was bouncing up and down, and every few bounces flapping his wings and lifting from the ground. It was apparent that Dracon was having a great time.

The dragon pages were all sitting along the edge of the field, watching their respective dragons enjoy their time with all the others. Kadil looked up and saw Merlin and Aeem approaching. He stood up and began walking toward the two of them.

"That is quite some dragon you have there, Merlin," he said as Merlin got close enough to hear him. "I have never seen a dragon that learns as fast as he does."

"His father and mother were quite special. It has nothing to do with me."

"Well, I am sure that you have helped in encouraging him to use his talents wisely."

Upon landing from one of his flights into the air, Dracon looked over and saw Merlin at the side of the field.

He spread his wings wide and flapped them against the air, lifting him quickly off the ground. He flew over to where Merlin was standing and landed gracefully in front of Merlin, Aeem, and Kadil.

"I see you have made a few friends," Merlin said to Dracon.

Dracon blinked his eyes, as he always had done with Merlin, to indicate his answer. However, this time, Merlin was in for a big surprise.

"Yes. Friends."

Dracon had just spoken his first words to Merlin. It was apparent that Dracon was doing more than just learning more aerial maneuvers and how to run, dodge, and jump from his little dragon friends. This was truly a great milestone in Dragon's life.

"Dracon! You're talking!" Merlin said with great joy.

"Yes. Talking."

"He started doing that just before lunch." Kadil informed Merlin. "He picks up on almost every word said to him. Usually, the young dragons say a word, then it's a day or so later before they say another one."

"All of the young dragons that were raised in the valley where I grew up left before they started to talk. I have never been around one when he is just starting to speak. Dracon is the first."

"Dracon first. Merlin's dragon." Dracon said.

"Yes. Dracon is Merlin's dragon. I am very proud of you Dracon. Your father would be proud too," Merlin said to Dracon.

"Father. Proud," Dracon said as he looked up toward the sky as if knowing that his father was not of this world.

Merlin, Aeem, and Kadil all looked up toward the sky as well. They all knew that the spirit of Dracon's father was somewhere in the cosmos, and he was probably aware of his son's accomplishments thus far, in this realm of the life cycle where they dwelled.

As they all lowered their heads, they looked around at each other, happy that they all had the opportunity to be a part of each other's life.

"Dracon, you can go back with your friends and play. I have something very important I need to do," Merlin said as he looked off toward the Mountains of Amazmond.

Once again, Dracon spread his wings out wide and lifted from the ground as he brushed his wings against the air around him. Merlin and Dracon's eyes were fixed on each other until the young dragon turned to go back to the field where the other dragons were playing.

"Thanks for all you are doing to make Dragon's stay here a pleasant one," Merlin said to Kadil.

"It is my duty. However, it is also a great pleasure to be able to serve as Dracon's page while he is here. It is something I shall keep in my memory all of my life. If you will pardon me, I will return now to my station with the other pages."

Kadil bowed his head to Merlin, then turned and walked away.

Aeem knew exactly what Merlin was going to say next. She pointed to the right from where they were standing and said, "The field and the dragon that you seek is over there. There are some things I need to attend to as well. I will see you later this afternoon, before dinner. I wish you much success in your attempt to negotiate the passage through the mountains. I know how dangerous it is, however, I believe in your ability to make it safely through."

Merlin was not sure why, but rather than curtsy before turning to leave, Aeem leaned toward Merlin and kissed him on the cheek. Again, this was not one of those times for Merlin to complain about such an action.

He watched as Aeem walked away toward the castle and disappeared around some bushes along the pathway. He slowly raised his hand and touched his cheek where Aeem had placed the kiss. Smiling, he too turned in the direction Aeem had pointed and headed off to find the dragon he was to ride on the morrow.

Chapter Twelve

The Final Practice Run

Rounding a corner along one of the castle walls, Merlin recognized the gardens that he walked through a couple of times before. There behind the gardens was the labyrinth of hedges, which he had gone through to watch the stars with Aeem. Merlin knew which way to go to reach the meadow where the dragon, which he had ridden earlier that day, would be resting.

He walked briskly through the gardens and turned left just as he reached the labyrinth, knowing that, within minutes, he would arrive at the field. It would not be long now until he would be negotiating the pass through the mountains as he had done earlier that day. He was already starting to devise a plan in his head about how he would approach the dangerous course. There were a few places through the path of the race, in which he thought he could gain a few minutes, and he could see in his mind's eye how he would improve upon his earlier performance.

Running up the side of the grassy ledge that surrounded the field, Merlin got to the top of the hill, and there, waiting for him in the grassy meadow was a lone dragon. The dragon saw Merlin just as he topped the crest of the mound and he gave a snort from his nostrils. The dragon too was anxious to negotiate the mountains again, with his rider astride him.

As Merlin ran through the grass of the meadow, the dragon watched, knowing that with each step Merlin took they were both that much closer to lifting into the air. Just before Merlin reached him, the dragon lowered one wing to the ground so that Merlin would be able to climb atop his back the moment that he got there.

Merlin jumped high into the air just as he approached the dragon, landing just behind the dragon's neck. He grabbed the rope that was wrapped about the dragon's neck, just as he had done earlier. It was just in time too, because as he landed on the dragon's back, the dragon raised and with one swoop of his wing's lifted high into the air. They bolted off in the direction of the Mountains of Amazmond in a flash.

It might have been that the dragons were all taking it easy on Merlin through the first trip, earlier on, because it seemed he was moving much faster than they had before. However, Merlin was prepared in his mind for a much better performance this time around and was ready to meet each maneuver of the dragon with some tricks of his own. This time, Merlin would be working much more in harmony with the moves of the dragon to get through this much faster than before.

Merlin remembered almost every turn and opening along the way, through the treacherous mountains, and was not going to be surprised like he was before. Moreover, he didn't have the distraction of watching what the other riders were doing ahead of him to sway him from planning how best to get through the treacherous situations.

Similar to earlier in the day, as they approached the pass leading into the mountains, Merlin moving quickly, saw the opening. Merlin knew what he must do to make it through the passage alive, but held his position upright to coax the dragon to use every swoop of his wings to maintain their speed toward the opening.

Then at the very last moment, he leaned forward, clutching the dragon closely, at which point the dragon pulled his wings back and turned to make it through the opening. Immediately after they made it through the pass, the dragon turned back upright and stretched his wings, flapping them against the wind, increasing their speed even more.

Having passed through the dragon's gate, one of the troll overlord's spies returned to the refuge of the overlord to report to the findings of his cohorts. One of the overlord's associates announced the spies' arrival and he was given entrance to the inner chamber of the overlord.

"Do you have some good news for me?" The overlord questioned.

"Yes my lord. We found the one who entered the Tome. He is a guest of the Dragon Lord. It appears he will be returning to where he came from shortly though. His stay is only temporary."

"Good!" The overlord roared.

There was silence for a few seconds. Then the overlord gave the spy new instructions. As soon as he was done, the scout once again left the chambers of the overlord to return to his cohorts, back in the world of the Dragon Lord.

"As soon as Merlin returns to the castle, have him brought to me so I can speak with him," the Dragon Lord instructed one of the chambermaids.

The chambermaid bowed to the Dragon Lord, then turned and exited the room.

Elsewhere in the castle, Aeem was again standing at the window, watching for Merlin to come over the mountaintop, as she had done earlier that morning. She had watched him disappear in the midst of the mountains when he had left the meadows behind the castle and had rushed to the window where she was now, just as before. Her gaze was fixed on the mountain ledge high above, waiting breathlessly for him to return.

In the Mountains of Amazmond, Merlin was negotiating the passes and tunnels along the way with much greater ease than he had done before. He was sure he was making much better time and was going to fly over the final mountaintop, ready to swoop down toward the finish line below.

As he recognized the final turn along the raceway, he knew that they would be going through the mountains and that the dragon would be flying almost straight up to go over the peak that majestically watched over the castle below. He suddenly became conscious that there were probably others who he would be racing against, that would be waiting to see him come over the mountaintop. Since he knew he was making it through the course much faster than before; he did not want to give away his alacrity so that others could know what they would have to do to beat his time.

As he leaned to one side, moving close to the dragon, the dragon spread his wings out wide and they made the turn around the final bend. However, when the dragon started to flap his wings to make the climb over the mountain, Merlin pulled on the rope indicating to the dragon that he wanted him to hold back. Merlin guided the dragon to a ledge directly below the mountaintop and had the dragon land there just below the final ridge.

From the window of the castle, Aeem watched, feeling that any minute Merlin would come over the mountaintop. She was sure he would appear much sooner than before, as she believed Merlin would do much better the second time around.

There were others watching as well. Just as Merlin had anticipated, some of the others who were to be in the race were waiting to see how Merlin would do through the course. As all eyes focused on the mountaintop, there was no sign of Merlin. Even as time passed, when he should have appeared, there was still no trace of the young man or his dragon mount.

Aeem was starting to worry, wondering why Merlin had not appeared. She started to think something must have gone wrong. Did he get hurt trying to improve upon his speed? Was he lying helpless on some mountain ledges along the way? Surely if Merlin had gotten hurt the dragon would have returned to get someone to help.

Merlin didn't realize that his move to mislead the other racers about his speed through the course was also making someone else worry a great deal. When Aeem had told Merlin that she had something to do, he was not aware that "something" was going to entail standing at the castle window to watch him disappear in the distance, and then wait for his return over the final mountaintop.

Even the other riders had started to become concerned about Merlin, wondering what was holding him up. There was, however, one in the kingdom that knew what Merlin was up to. For just as before, the Dragon Lord was actively waiting at his window looking for Merlin. Nevertheless, unlike everyone else, the Dragon Lord knew Merlin was far too wise to allow anyone in the kingdom to know of that which he was capable. The Dragon Lord watched, knowing any second Merlin would come over the grandiose mountain, which stood next to the castle.

A dragon came bursting over the mountaintop just as everyone had anticipated, but so much later than what anyone had expected. There on top of the dragon, his rider could be seen, leaning close to the dragon's back, coaxing him to fly swiftly to the finish line.

With a sigh of relief, Aeem put her hand to her mouth and closed her eyes, holding back the tears that had welled up inside her lower eyelids. She was so thankful to see Merlin return and was now able to go take care of the things she needed to do before going to get Merlin for dinner.

Just as Merlin and his dragon passed the place where the finish of the race would take place, the dragon swooped up into the air and turned toward the castle, flying over it with a great showing of skill and speed. The two had definitely bonded and were now a team with which to be reckoned!

Chapter Thirteen

Another Gift from the King

As Merlin and his racing dragon landed in the meadow, there was someone there to meet them. It was the person who had greeted Merlin and Aeem when they returned from the city just after noon. Merlin knew before the person spoke that the King was sending for him. He slid down the side of the dragon and landed firmly on the ground.

"I am sorry to see that your run through the mountains did not go well for you." The messenger said to Merlin.

Merlin knew straight away that he had succeeded in hiding the true account of his trek through the mountains. He knew that he could not tell a soul about how well he had done lest he gave away everything.

"I can only hope to do better during the race," Merlin said, holding back the truth of the matter.

"The King would like to have your appearance in his chambers at this time." The messenger said to Merlin, bowing his head slightly.

"I shall follow your lead," Merlin said to the king's messenger. Then he turned to the dragon and said, "I shall see you on the morrow. I am sure we can do much better." He winked at the dragon with one eye as they both knew well that Merlin had pulled off a great deception.

"Until tomorrow." The dragon replied.

The king's messenger turned and headed toward the castle, Merlin following close behind him.

Knocking at the door to the Dragon Lord's chambers, his messenger awaited the King's voice before opening the door.

"Enter," called a deep voice from within the king's chambers.

Upon this cue, the messenger opened the door to the chambers and stood to one side indicating to Merlin that he entered the room. After Merlin entered through the doorway, the messenger closed the door behind him. The envoy then left, walking down the hallway leaving Merlin to visit with the King alone as was the King's request.

The chambers of the Dragon Lord were quite spacious. The furnishings were what one would expect in size for someone of his great stature. The woodwork in the room was as magnificent as any Merlin had ever seen before. The grandeur of the ceiling overhead was splendorous as well, as it was patterned with paintings depicting different scenes in each segment. The walls were filled with the most beautiful and colorful frieze one might ever have the chance to cast their eyes upon.

"That was quite something that you did on that run through the mountains," the King said to Merlin.

"You know?" Merlin asked, amazed.

"I did not get to where I am by holding back on any of my senses. To become a Dragon Lord one must know oneself as well as know as much about everything that is around them as is possible. You have the makings of a great leader. In addition, sometimes great leaders sit in counsel to those who are called to be the head over others. There are many things you are not and among these things are being complacent or slothful."

Merlin was starting to think that the Dragon Lord knew more about him than he knew about himself. He was hopeful that in time he could only know a portion of what the great dragon knew.

"Even now, while your wisdom is much greater than that of others your age, your modesty matches your acumen. Pride is the destroyer of those who could rise to great heights of leadership. Those who rise the highest are those who understand they are nothing more than anyone else. We are all equal as far as the consciousness of creation. To be a great leader one must also be able to follow, and those who make poor followers are even worse as leaders. You have the makings of both a good follower and a great leader. Never let your education get in the way of your learning. The universe has an endless multitude of secrets to share with those who have a mind open to learning what is within and without it. Your journey is just beginning, and no journey ever has an end. There are just more doors that lead to other realms where there is even more, to learn and to gain experience from. Life is endless, not finite as some would have others believe. Where one door closes there is always something on the other side that is a realm into another universe of erudition."

The Dragon Lord stopped speaking to give Merlin time to contemplate the things he had just said. Merlin stood motionless, realizing that the person whom he was in the presence of was wiser than anyone he had ever known. While he remembered sitting in a room with the Wizer, back in the valley, and listening to him share his insights and feeling so good about the words he spoke, the words which he was now hearing come forth from this great Dragon Lord made his heart swell with joy even more.

"I have somewhere I want to take you." The Dragon Lord walked closer to where Merlin was standing. He gave a small gesture with his hand as if strumming an instrument. A bright light enveloped the two of them and they disappeared from the king's chambers.

When Merlin and the King reappeared, they were standing on a ledge on the side of a huge mountain. There was a vast gorge below and mountains on either side surrounded them. It was quite a breathtaking view.

The Dragon Lord turned toward the mountain and started walking toward the wall of stone. Merlin followed him as he was sure that was what the King intended for him to do. As the two of them were just about to walk right into the stony side of the mountain, they were pulled right into it, disappearing from the ledge upon which they had arrived.

On the other side of the stone wall, the Dragon Lord and Merlin appeared in a cosmic cavern. It appeared to be as endless as the sky at night. The inside of the cavern was filled with innumerable crystals, gems, and stones, which glittered from every direction as far as the eye can see. This great sea of gemstones lit the cavern up like it was being filled with the light of the noonday sun.

Elfins were coming and going in the cavern as if there were doors leading into it from every direction possible. Each time an Elfin entered the cavern, it placed a gemstone somewhere among the others in the cave.

"Every time a dragon ceases to breathe somewhere in the universe, upon its last breath a gemstone is left in its place which contains the quintessence of the dragon's physical life. While the spirit of the dragon goes to another realm, the personification of the dragon's physical life is left in the gemstone that remains where he took his last breath. From time before till now, this cavern contains the gemstone of every dragon that has lived on every world in the cosmos. The Elfins collect the gemstones and bring them here, where they remain until they will again be reunited with the spirit of the dragon from which they came. In the meantime, the spirits of all those who have lived in the physical realm, such as we know it, are in another realm where they continue to learn and grow. All life, no matter what form it may take; exists in order to develop to a higher level. There are those in the universe who would seek to destroy all life as we know it and the life yet to be had. There are others who are the protectors of this life and who seek to help to allow the life not yet known to come about. That which is to be cannot be destroyed no matter what evil may attempt to get in its way."

Merlin looked all about the cavern. He was in awe at how beautiful it all was. The colorful shining gemstones that surrounded him were once part of the life of a dragon who had lived somewhere on some world in some part of the universe. He wondered how many worlds there could be in the universe. There appeared to be millions upon millions of gemstones in the cavern surrounding him. So many had already lived and died somewhere in this universe. How many more were still living now, and how many more are yet to live?

"A long time ago, the first dragon visited your world and found that it was good. The decision was made to build a gate so that others could also visit your world as well. These gates exist in worlds all throughout the universe.

There are others in the cosmos that have discovered how to use the gates to gain access to the worlds where they exist. When those of one world would seek to do harm to those of another world where they are defenseless against such evil, it is an event that calls for the destruction of that gate."

Merlin recalled that when he entered the Tome he appeared at such a gate in his world. The time had already come when the dragon's gate there had been destroyed. Someone had made the decision to destroy it but who and why?

"Hold out your hands," the Dragon Lord said as he put his hand out.

Merlin raised his arms to the square with his palms up. Again the Dragon Lord moved his fingers, as he had done before. This time Merlin's staff appeared in hands.

"I have something to give you. It will help you along your journey. This gift I desire to bestow upon you contains the power to create or to destroy. You must use this gift wisely. Never take another life, except in defending your own or in protecting that of another."

The Dragon Lord held out his hand toward the center of the cavern. All the gemstones in the grotto began to light up. Beams of light began coming forth from all the gemstones, in the direction of the Dragon Lord's hand. As the beams of light began to coalesce just above the King's hand, an object began to form. The light was so bright that Merlin could barely keep his eyes open. Suddenly all the beams of light burst forth like a swarm of fireflies drifting across the meadow. Then the beams ceased. There, in the hand of the Dragon Lord, was a beautiful gemstone that shone with every color of the rainbow. It was glowing as if alive.

"Hand me your staff," the Dragon Lord instructed Merlin.

Merlin stretched out his arm, with the staff in hand, and gave it to the Dragon Lord. The Dragon Lord placed the gemstone in the slot at the top of the staff and then touched the top of it with the claw at the end of one of his fingers.

The wood about the opening swelled slightly, locking the gemstone into place. The Dragon Lord then handed the staff back to Merlin. Just as the staff switched hands the gemstone glowed with a brilliant burst of colors, then went dim when the Dragon Lord let go of it, releasing it to Merlin.

"This is a Spirita Stone. It contains a portion of the essence of all the dragons whose gemstones surround these cavern walls. It is something I give to you to help you because there are many trials you will face along your journey. There are many evil ones who will wish to do you harm because of the things you will be able to do for the people of your world. Dragons will not always walk freely upon your earth. There is an evil that will come upon your world that will demand that dragons can no longer walk there. Though we have the power to destroy any evil, we must allow every world to determine its own destiny. Do not fret though. As long as there are always men and women in your world who believe in liberty and are willing to defend it; good will always prevail."

With those final words, the Dragon Lord again waved his fingers and Merlin appeared in his room inside the castle.

Merlin went to the window and looked out over the kingdom below. There were so many creatures and people from so many planets and he felt humbled that among all that existed, he had been honored with such things as had been given him by the Dragon Lord. Nevertheless, he also knew that with such great gifts came great responsibility. It was a responsibility, he hoped, he would always meet with honor.

Chapter Fourteen

Festival Eve

Kadil was escorting Dracon back to Merlin's quarters when the two of them crossed paths with Aeem, who was on her way to the room to get Merlin and Dracon for the evening's festivities. The three of them walked together along the halls of the castle. When they reached the door to Merlin's quarters, Aeem knocked softly at the door and then slowly began opening it to enter the room.

As the three of them entered, Merlin came walking out of the sleeping area to the quarters, smiling from ear to ear.

Aeem, seeing that Merlin was very happy about something asked, "What are you smiling about?"

"I am just very happy to see the three of you."

Merlin was holding his staff, which did not go unnoticed by Dracon. He could sense some kind of aura coming from the staff, which was not there before. Dracon walked over to where Merlin was standing and eyed the staff from top to bottom. Then his eyes became fixed on the top of the staff. He began looking closely at the stone, which he noticed was new.

Aeem and Kadil, now noticing the stone as well, walked over to Merlin and began admiring the new addition to his staff.

"What is it?" Aeem asked.

"It is a gift from the King. It is called a Spirita Stone."

"A Spirita Stone!" Kadil exclaimed. "There has not been such as one like this in a very long time. When used properly, they are very powerful. But, if used for evil, it can turn against the one who tries to use it for such."

All of them were fixated on the stone. Its beautiful colors were so alluring and for a brief second, it appeared to glow. It was as if the stone was speaking to the four of them. Merlin, Aeem, and Kadil could feel a sudden sense of peace and well-being fall upon them.

Dracon was especially drawn to the stone. He could sense something more about it. He felt a sensation of kinship but he didn't quite know why.

"Friend." Dracon said.

Merlin realized that Dracon must have been sensing the spirit of all the dragons that the stone encompassed. In this stone was the essence of his ancestors. Merlin stretched out his arm and placed the end of the staff against the side of Dragon's head. The Spirita Stone glowed brightly. It was as though the gemstone was speaking to Dracon. A tear formed in the corner of Dragon's eye.

Merlin, Aeem, and Kadil stood quietly allowing Dracon to relish the moment. Aeem and Kadil knew what a Spirita Stone was, and how one came about. They had heard stories about these stones before. This was the very first time they had ever had the opportunity to see one. For them, it was a great occasion as well.

After a few moments, Dracon raised his head and looked at the three.

"Love." Dracon said tenderly.

"Yes. Love" agreed Merlin.

"Love," Aeem said.

Kadil nodded his head in agreement.

The stone went dim and Merlin lowered the staff from Dragon's head. They all looked around at each other smiling.

It wasn't his intention to break the spirit of the moment, but Merlin was curious. "I notice there is a lot of activity around the castle and down in the city," Merlin said.

Aeem replied, "This is festival eve. It is the time of the great celebration the night before the Celestial Fête. Of course, you and Dracon are invited. Everyone will be expecting you. Kadil will personally escort Dracon for the evening and see to it that he finds his way to the other young dragons attending the night's activities."

"Is there anything special I need to wear?" Merlin questioned.

"Not really. You might want to freshen up a bit. Anything you choose to wear will be fine."

"Give me a few minutes to get ready."

Merlin swiftly went back into the sleeping quarters and into the lavatory to clean up and change clothes.

While Merlin was in the back room getting ready, Kadil took care to ready Dragon's sleeping area so that when Dracon returned later that night he could nestle up for a good night's rest for the games the next day.

Aeem thought this would be a good time to sing Dracon a song. After all, she was Dracon's dragon maiden and as such, was responsible for ensuring his comfort. She reached into a small pouch that hung from her side and took something out of it. It was a small flute-like instrument. She put it close to her lips and blew a few notes as a prelude to her song.

On dragon's wings above the clouds

One can soar beyond the crowds

Solitary sky above one's head

No toil or trouble nor evil dread.

You spread your wings against the wind

You deem all life your dearest friend

Soar higher than the highest peak

Guardian of the mild and meek.

Honor and might, which you possess

Paramount love your eyes confess

Dragon's heart virtue of our cosmic sphere

Where dragons dwell there's naught to fear.

Merlin, having freshened up and a change of clothes, had come back to the room where Aeem and Dracon were. He stood quietly behind Aeem and listened attentively.

As Aeem continued her song, Merlin remembered how his mother would sing to him. Tears began to form in the corner of Merlin's eyes as he missed his mother very much. Images of her ran through his mind reminding him of all the fond memories he held of her. In his heart, he hoped that soon he would see her again.

Aeem finished her song. As she was putting the instrument back into the pouch on her side, she caught a glimpse of Merlin out of one corner of her eye. She looked up at him just as he was wiping his eyes to hide the tears.

"Are you alright?"

"Yes. I was just thinking about my mother. Your song brought images into my mind of her."

"I am sure you miss her a great deal. I believe that Keltos will not mind my sharing this with you. He is planning to take you back to your world after the fête tomorrow. This will be your last night here."

Merlin was now feeling a bit confused. While he missed his mother and wanted to see her, he had grown attached to Aeem and when he returned to his world knew that he would now miss her.

"Let's enjoy the time you have left and the festivities of this night and the games tomorrow," Aeem suggested to Merlin, smiling.

Merlin knew Aeem was right. Why worry about what was to happen on the morrow when there were more precious memories that could be made at this very moment.

Aeem took the lead and walked to the door. As she opened the door she said, "Let's all go have a great time."

Following Aeem's suggestion, Merlin headed for the door. Dracon and Kadil followed close behind him. Aeem closed the door and the four of them left the refuge of the castle.

There was dancing and singing and a myriad of other activities going on outside the walls of the castle. There were tables all around the streets and everyone was helping themselves to the wide array of foods that were on hand. Merlin was getting hungry and was all too ready to start helping himself to the food as well.

"I am going to take Dracon to the area where the other young dragons are," Kadil said to Merlin.

Merlin turned and looked at Dracon and said, "Have fun Dracon. Do not worry about me. I will be alright."

Dracon looked in the direction of Aeem and gave his little dragon smile. He knew that Merlin was going to be more than just alright.

With those words, Kadil turned to go off down the street and Dracon quickly turned to follow him.

Aeem took Merlin by the hand and led him into the crowd of people.

There was someone trying to follow the two of them but he lost them immediately after Aeem and Merlin entered the swarm of people.

As the evening progressed, Aeem and Merlin continued to mingle among the crowd and enjoy the food and games. Merlin was sampling every kind of food he possibly could. It was not every day one had such a vast array of food put before them and Merlin was, after all, a growing boy.

As the sky began to get dark and the stars began to shine in the sky overhead, every now and then there would be a loud bang above them, and colorful starry-like objects shot out in all directions from where the explosion took place, up in the air. Merlin had never seen fireworks. He did not know how he could ever explain something like this to his friends back home.

Just as Merlin finished the last bite of something he had picked up from one of the tables, he and Aeem were rounding a bend in the street where there was a group of musicians playing music. Some of the people among the crowd were dancing merrily in the street just in front of the musicians.

Aeem took Merlin's hand. She pulled him over to the area where the people were dancing. She began to dance. At first, Merlin stood there unsure of what to do. He had never danced before. He watched a few of the other boys that were dancing and started to imitate what they were doing. It was not long before Merlin himself was moving his legs to the rhythm of the music and doing quite well.

Merlin and Aeem were unaware that someone was watching them. The stranger that had tried to follow them earlier on had now found them and was keeping a close eye on them. It was the overload's spy. He was keeping his distance but nonetheless was determined to get the information his master had sent him to obtain.

The two of them continued to dance for quite some time. Once in a while, they would stop to catch their breath and get something to drink from the vendors. The fireworks continued to explode overhead. Music continued to play all throughout the square, and people and other creatures were coming and going all throughout the evening. Except for a glance now and then at what was going on around him, Merlin, for the most part, was oblivious to what was happening in the square. He was enjoying this time with Aeem and making the most of every second he had with her.

When it was almost midnight, Aeem knew the time had come when she needed to get Merlin back to the castle so he could get a good night's sleep so as to be rested for the competitions and games on the morrow. She took Merlin by the hand and led him away from where they were dancing. They made their way slowly out of the crowd heading toward the castle.

The overload's spy followed close behind but was inconspicuous just the same.

As they were walking, Aeem made a confession to Merlin. "I am going to miss you when you leave tomorrow."

"Me too," Merlin replied.

"I know you will be very happy to return to your world."

"I am going to miss everything about your world here. I will always remember everything, including you."

As the two of them continued toward the castle, the overload's spy backed away. He had heard what he had come to find out and would now return to the overlord with the information.

Chapter Fifteen

Good Luck Kiss

When Merlin and Aeem arrived at his quarters, they found Dracon sound asleep. They quietly slipped past him and went out onto the balcony, overlooking the gardens and labyrinth. It was quiet now as everyone attending the festivities for the evening had all gone. The stars in the sky beamed brightly overhead, and it was one of the most beautiful nights ever to behold.

At first, the two of them just stared upwards into the darkness of the sky, not saying a word. It was as though neither of them knew exactly what to say considering the fact that on the morrow Merlin would be returning to his world.

Then finally, Aeem broke the silence by saying, "I wish I could see your world. I am sure it is very pretty there. And I would love to meet your parents and all your friends there."

"I wish you could too," Merlin replied.

"Sometimes wishes do come true." Aeem asserted.

Merlin was hoping, in his heart of hearts, that this would be one of those times when a wish would come true.

Aeem felt it would be best to change the subject to something much nearer at hand. "Are you ready for the big race tomorrow?"

"I think so."

"You know, the other racers have done this many times before and have a great deal of experience. They are going to be fierce competition."

"I am a little nervous about it; however, I will just do the best I can."

"That is all one can really do," Aeem said, agreeing with Merlin. Then she added, "I have something you can do that will help you greatly. I know the most important thing is not that you come in first in the race, but rather that you are able to participate in it, and that you are able to finish without any unfortunate mishap. I am going to share with you something that will give you the necessary power that will help you make it through it. Perhaps it is something that can help you to be victorious over everyone else."

Merlin was curious as to what Aeem could give him, which would provide him with some kind of advantage over the others in the race. In addition, he was sure that someone of Aeem's nature would never give him something that could be considered cheating.

"What is it?" Merlin asked.

"Close your eyes."

At first, Merlin hesitated and gave Aeem a look of wonderment. He trusted her so he did as she requested and closed both eyes.

"Take a couple of deep breaths, and relax."

Again, Merlin followed Aeem's instructions and took a few deep breaths, allowing himself to relax with each one.

"As you relax, see yourself standing at the center of everyone, following the race. One and all are cheering and congratulating you for having won."

Merlin could see in his mind's eye the image that Aeem was portraying him in words. He continued to breathe slowly and listened to Aeem as she spoke.

"You look around in every direction, seeing the smiles and you can hear them cheering."

As Aeem spoke to Merlin he continued to see the images. He could actually create the sounds in his mind, as well as see the cheering people in front of him. It made him feel good, and it was as though it was actually happening.

"See yourself now getting off the dragon as he lands among the crowd." Aeem waited for just a few seconds to give Merlin time to create the image in his mind. "Back up one more moment and see yourself crossing the finish line, just ahead of everyone else." Again, she gave him a second to see it. "See yourself negotiating the racecourse and jockeying for a good position to head for the finish line. Finally, see yourself leaving the starting line as the signal is given for the race to start."

One last time Aeem stopped to give Merlin time to create the images of what she was saying in his mind.

"When you are ready, open your eyes."

Merlin took one final breath and then opened his eyes as Aeem had suggested. He was amazed at how much more relaxed he was about the impending race. He felt a calm come over him, and a new sense of confidence about how he would do in the race. Most of all, it really did not matter to him whether he would actually come in first in the race. He just had a good feeling now about being a part of it.

Aeem could sense what Merlin was feeling. She knew she had given Merlin a nice gift, which he could use for anything in life he would have to face.

"One of the keys to achieving great things in life is our ability to believe in what it is we are going to do. If our confidence is lacking and we do not really have a strong belief in what it is we are doing or going to do, we will not do well in it. On the other hand, if we instill in our minds the confidence that we will do well, or even more so, that we will be great, then the probability is that we will do much better than we would without that assurance."

Merlin understood exactly what Aeem was saying because he could feel a difference in the way he felt about the coming race. He was much more relaxed and he was sure that no matter what happened, he was already a winner.

"You will also need to get a good night's sleep, so it is best I go now," Aeem said as she smiled at Merlin. The smile was returned in kind.

"Oh, one last thing I want to give you." Aeem leaned toward Merlin and gave him a kiss. This time it was not on the cheek.

Of all the firsts in life that Merlin had experienced so far, this was truly the greatest.

Aeem turned and headed toward the door to the quarters. Merlin watched as she opened the door and disappeared, closing it behind her.

This was truly the best moment of his life thus far. He walked back into the room, closed the door to the balcony, and went to the sleeping quarters.

As Merlin lay down for the last night of sleep there in the world of the Dragon Lord, he closed his eyes, took a few deep breaths, and began rehearsing images in his mind as he had done as Aeem spoke the words to him. Only this time, he was seeing a different set of images of something he wanted very much to come true.

Chapter Sixteen

Morning of the Fête

The sky was clear and blue as the sun came up over the horizon. It was a perfect day for the Celestial Fête. As the light of the sun began to pour over the kingdom and all about the castle of the Dragon Lord, people, and creatures all began to wake ready for one of the most exciting days that occurs in the known universe. Moreover, as is the custom with each day, Dracon was up early. He was waiting for Kadil to arrive and escort him to the royal kitchen for his breakfast.

What was different about this day as opposed to other days was that Merlin had awakened before Dracon and was already prepared to go have breakfast. Merlin emerged from the doorway leading into his sleeping quarters and greeted Dracon with a hearty greeting.

"Good morning Dracon!"

Dracon turned his head to see Merlin walking toward him much to his surprise. He could not think of a day when

Merlin had ever awakened before him. What had gotten into him?

"Merlin OK?" Dracon asked.

"Merlin is more than OK," he replied.

As was expected, it was not long before there was a knock at the door. The door opened and in walked Kadil with a bucket of water and cloth as he had done the day before. He immediately freshened up Dracon, while Merlin watched the cleaning process. Once he was done, he escorted Dracon to the kitchen as well, however, this time Merlin went along.

When they arrived at the kitchen, the royal chef was there to welcome them as he had done the day before.

"Ah, Dracon! Et Merlin," The jolly old royal chef said, greeting the two of them. "I have prepared for you something quite special for you."

In the royal kitchen, every meal is considered quite special. The royal chef knew, however, that by always being so jolly and enjoying each day by greeting those who attended his galley with a smile, it was the perfect milieu for making a meal more appetizing. Moreover, it made the work that he did more enjoyable as well.

After the royal kitchen servers placed food before Merlin and Dracon, the royal chef bowed deeply, and then said "Benu pleazur". He then turned, departing for the kitchen.

Once Merlin and Dracon were partaking of their morning meal, Kadil bid farewell so that he could attend to his other duties.

"I will find the two of you later so that I can take Dracon to the place where he will be starting in the race." Kadil informed Merlin. He then nodded his head to Merlin then turned and departed.

It was only a few minutes when the royal chef came back into the galley and stood looking at the front door. Within a matter of seconds, Aeem entered through the door and the royal chef greeted her. "Ah, Aeem! I have prepared you something quite special." Moreover, as always he added his jolly smile along with the greeting.

Aeem took a seat at the table with Merlin and the royal servers immediately came in with the meal that the jolly chef had prepared for her. It amazed Merlin that the royal chef seemed to know before somebody entered the galley that they were about to enter and that he had prepared each individual a special meal that was just for them. However, that thought did not hold his attention very long as the one person he was looking forward to seeing this day was Aeem. And here she was now sitting with him at the morning breakfast table.

As the royal servers departed, the royal chef said as always, "Benu pleazur". Then he left for the kitchen as well.

"Good morning, Aeem," Merlin said.

"Yes, it is a good morning," she replied.

The two of them talked about the big event of the day, which was the impending race. Before the race was to take place though, there was to be a royal parade and carnival. The royal race would be the final event of the fête.

"Before I went to sleep last night, I too created images in my mind of you crossing the finish line before everyone else." Aeem shared with Merlin.

"I had a reverie of my own," replied Merlin. He did not however tell Aeem what his meditation was about.

"It is good to reflect on the things that you desire in your mind, as it starts to create the reality of it. Since thought is the very seed of all reality, the more you nourish a thought, the more probable it is that it will become reality.

And when two people are focused on the same goal, it creates an essence of making reality even more probable."

"So by you helping create the image of me winning the race then my chances are greatly increased. Is that right?" Merlin asked.

"Yes."

"What if I mess up or something?"

"Just keep saying to yourself... 'No matter what happens, I am crossing the finish line first.' Your subconscious will guide you toward doing what is necessary. This is more than a race of just power and strength, it is a race of wits. The one, who believes the most and has the strongest desire to win, will come out the victor."

"I will work on that throughout the rest of this day and throughout the race," Merlin said.

When the three of them finished their morning meal, they left the galley to go outside the castle to take part in the carnival and get ready for the parade.

Chapter Seventeen

The Royal Parade

All throughout the kingdom, there was a flurry of activity. As the night before, people were dancing and celebrating. In addition, there were street vendors with games for the young to play and other activities that everyone could take part in. There were jugglers, acrobats, and entertainers of all types performing.

One of the first things that Aeem, Dracon, and Merlin came upon was a huge pole, with the head of a dragon at the top, and a bell hanging from his neck. Not a real dragon's head mind you, but a replica of a dragon's head. The vendor handed Merlin a huge hammer and challenged him to give it a try.

"Here you go, son. See if you can ring the bell."

Merlin took the hammer in hand. He pulled together every bit of energy he had and took a swing at the lever that catapulted the object up toward the bell. The object went just over halfway up the poll and then came sliding back down.

"Come now. A boy as big as you can do better than that." The vendor coaxed him.

Merlin again took a deep breath and swung as hard as he could at the lever. Again, the object slid up the poll this time going a bit further up the poll, then it returned again.

Merlin closed his eyes and concentrated. He saw the object hitting the bell. Then he opened his eyes and gave another swing at the lever.

The object went up toward the top of the poll just barely touching the bell, making it cling slightly. It wasn't a resounding cling, however, one that was audible.

Aeem applauded.

Merlin turned and smiled at her. He then handed the vendor the hammer. The vendor reached over to a shelf to one side and took a prize from it. He handed it to Merlin and said,

"Congratulations."

Merlin accepted the prize from him and then handed it to Aeem.

Just as the three of them were about to go further down the street, Kadil came walking up to them.

"I know some things that Dracon would like to do," Kadil said to Merlin and Aeem.

"Go have fun", Merlin said to Dracon.

"Dracon, have fun," Dracon replied.

Kadil nodded, then turned and started to walk back in the direction from where he had come, and Dracon followed him.

All morning long, Aeem and Merlin enjoyed the festival activities. They took a ride on a boat that went over the pond, and through a series of caverns. While they were riding, occasionally a mermaid or merman would swim up to the boat to get a closer look at Merlin. They had all heard about him, however, had not had the chance to get close to him until now.

Sometimes the younger mermaids would swim up to the boat in a group and then begin to giggle. If Merlin were a merman he would be fighting them off, as they were apparently finding him attractive, for a human that is.

The time was approaching for the big parade. People and creatures were lining the main street so as to watch the procession soon to come. Aeem and Merlin found what looked like a good place to sit for the parade.

It was almost noon when the parade was to start and both of them had not had anything to eat since their morning meal. A vendor approached with something that looked quite appetizing, so Aeem called out to him.

"Op dwy," Aeem shouted.

The vendor, hearing her, turned and went over to where Merlin and Aeem were seated.

"Dun ben?" He asked.

"Lui," replied Aeem.

The merchant handed Aeem two of the items from his tray. She gave him a coin and said, "Dit yo."

Just as the vendor took the coin, a voice could be heard just down the way, "Op dwy." The vendor looked toward where the voice came from and said, "Meplim." He tipped his head to Aeem and Merlin, then left to go serve the one calling him.

Handing one of the items of food to Merlin, they both began to eat. To a growing young man, such as he was, just about anything edible was agreeable with Merlin. Nevertheless, whatever this was, it was definitely met with his approval.

As usually happens when one eats though, it was just seconds when Merlin and Aeem both began to feel the need for something to drink. Aeem looked about and saw another vendor close by that was providing drinks.

She called out, "Op dwy."

There was no indication the vendor heard her so Aeem called out again.

"Op dwy."

This time the vendor heard her and quickly came over to where the two of them were.

"Dun ben?"

"Lui."

The vendor took two drinks from her container and handed one to Aeem and one to Merlin. Aeem gave the merchant a coin and as with the other vendor said, "Dit yo."

"Op dwy", someone called out. The vendor tipped her head to Aeem and said, "Dit yo." She then left.

Down the street, the first of those in the parade could be seen coming toward where Aeem and Merlin were seated. There were some acrobats who were coming down the street in the lead just before the parade. Everyone applauded as the tumblers went past doing the aerial tricks.

The excitement was mounting and everyone was enjoying the verity that the grand parade was underway. Everyone remained seated that were down the front so as not to block the view of those sitting further back. Most of the youngsters were upfront and they knew that those behind them would not be able to see the parade if they were to jump to their feet.

As the first of those in the parade began to pass by, the cheers became louder and everyone applauded the grand host and hostess who were on the first of the floats to pass by.

It was a spectacle to behold. Merlin had never seen a parade anything like this. The number of people that lived in the valley where he was from a parade would amount to a handful of floats and such and even then, there would be no one sitting along the side of the parade route watching.

The parade continued for well over an hour. There were all kinds of animals and creatures that passed by. While these were the usual passersby for those who had seen the parade before, everything was new to Merlin's eyes.

There were all the celebrities that warranted being called celebrities. Most all those being given recognition in the parade were because of some great achievement. However, as would be expected, the greatest of all the celebrities to pass by was now upon where Aeem and Merlin were seated.

For this particular person, everyone and every creature rose to their feet to pay homage. It was the Dragon Lord. Merlin could feel a sense of awe as the Dragon Lord passed by. For a moment, Merlin could tell that the King had actually looked over toward him and tipped his head at him.

There were so many memories of so many wonderful people and creatures and in such a short span of time that Merlin hoped in his heart he would remember all of this for the rest of his life.

As the final float passed by along the street, everyone began to disperse so as to go find the place they wanted to be when the grand race took place. Most everyone had someone or some creature they wanted to cheer on. The greatest race in the entire universe was about to begin.

Chapter Eighteen

A Grand Race

Every possible preparation had been made for the grand race, and all those that had come to watch the event had located a place to observe it. All those participating had taken their places at their respective starting points and were eager to get underway. Each group was being given their final instructions and the rules so that everyone participated fairly.

In the back of the castle, where the racing dragons were getting ready, Merlin and the other riders were learning of a change in the course they were to follow. The royal race master was speaking to all the dragon racers.

"Some of you have run this race prior to today's event. We are making a slight deviation in the course. This is to even the odds so that those that are racing for the first time have an equal chance of winning."

All of the riders looked around at each other. The riders who had been in the race before knew each other and what kind of competitor the other was. They did not feel the new riders would be much competition since they were not as used to the course. Now with the news of the change, the odds were in everyone's favor. Except for the fact that they had more experience, they would still have the task of figuring out what was the best course of action to take at every nook and cranny along the way.

"Here is a map showing you the new path. Your respective dragons have already had the opportunity to see this. Though your dragon will know his way through the course quite readily, it is up to you to guide your dragon through the course expediently. I wish all of you're the best of luck."

The royal race master then turned and left, as he had to start the race.

The racers looked over the map. Each of them began devising in their mind what they would do at certain portions of the racecourse where they felt they had the best chance of making a difference in the outcome. Merlin looked over the map and carefully charted in his mind as many of the obstacles and turns along the way as he could and the actions he would take in negotiating each of them. The only thing left to do now was to mount his dragon and take his position at the starting line to the leg of the race he was to run.

At the front of the castle, the fairies were all in a position to start the race. All along the racecourse, the other participants were also in place. The mermaids and mermen were ready as well as were the unicorns with their riders and the young dragons. The racing dragons were now all in their place in the field at the back of the castle.

The royal race master took his place at the starting booth. The spectators were all anxiously awaiting the signal. A hush descended all throughout the kingdom, as no one wanted to disturb the concentration of the fairies who were watching for the signal to begin.

The Dragon Lord was in a booth overlooking the grounds in front of the castle. Behind him were those who worked closely with him day-to-day. Roz was there with him along with Keltos, Aeem, and Kadil. The Dragon Lord nodded his head to the royal race master. The royal race master blew his horn indicating to all to make ready. He raised his starting flag high into the air. Participants and spectators alike held their breath in great anticipation. The royal race master suddenly dropped his arm, and they were off!

The fairies bolted from the starting line flying straight across the field in front of the castle. Everyone in the crowd cheered.

When the fairies reached the other side of the field, they turned left and started climbing high into the air heading toward the castle domes. They circled one of the domes and then headed for another. As they went around each of the domes, positions changed as some negotiated the turn better than the others. There was not only the task of remaining as close to the side of the dome as possible but also that of not being at the same level as one of the other fairies. When this happened, the fairy on the outside got pushed further away and had to fly further to get around the dome. The fairies all had to be quick-witted to outmaneuver all of the others racing against them.

Once they made the final turn around the second dome they flew down the roof-line at the back of the castle and down the castle wall toward the rose garden. There were obstacles in the rose garden that they had to pass through. They zigzagged their way through the gardens negotiating the obstacles along the way. Those that were observing around the garden area were now cheering the fairies on.

At the back of the gardens, the first of the fairies exited the gardens and entered the labyrinth. The path through the labyrinth was new, as during the night the royal gardeners had moved the hedges along the way, changing the exit. The fairies were very quick to catch on to this new route. Some of the fairies found themselves at a dead-end and immediately turned to go back the other way. Others would see the returning fairies and turn to follow them knowing there was no use in going further.

It was not long before the entire group of fairies had discovered the final path leading the way out, and they all were flying as speedily as they could to exit the labyrinth.

The fairies burst out from one side of the labyrinth and headed straight for the pond next to the castle. The mermaids were waiting for them along the water's edge.

Now, those who had been waiting nearby to watch this leg of the race were cheering and rooting the fairies on. The mermaids were each calling to the fairies to guide them to where they were in the waters.

The first of the fairies touched the top of the head of one of the mermaids, then the second, and so forth. The mermaids all began to swim toward the middle of the pond. There were hoops above the waters for the mermaids to jump through, and hoops under the water for them to swim through as well.

Seeing the mermaids jump the hoops above the water was quite a spectacle. Some of the hoops were just above the surface and they could jump through them by dipping slightly into the water and then leaping up through the hoop. Others were higher and the mermaids had to dive deep then swim quickly to the surface to jump high out of the water. In some cases, two and three mermaids would come up out of the water at the same time and pass through the hoops.

Their powerful tales moved in ways that Merlin could never have imagined. He was sure that they were moving faster than even the fastest ships in his world, in the harshest winds ever could. It was clear that the appendage was incredibly muscular, and could move with great force. He would not want to encounter an angry mer-person in the water.

As the mermaids passed through the final hoop, they began to swim to the other side of the pond where the mermen were sitting on the ledge along the water's edge waiting their turn. When the mermaids touched the wall next to the merman on their team, the merman would drop into the water and began swimming toward the middle of the pond.

There were no referees along the race path as everyone who participated adhered to the rules and guidelines to make the race as much fun as possible. They would not cheat as to do so was not honorable and anyone seen doing so would suffer shame. No one participating would dare put himself or herself through such anguish.

As the mermen got to the hoops, they burst out of the water and up through the first of them. There were hoops up high above the ones the mermaids jumped through and the mermen would dive deep into the pond passing through the hoops below the water then swimming as fast as they could to gain the speed needed to jump up out of the water to get through the higher hoops.

Some of them would do aerial maneuvers as they flew through the air toward the hoops adding to the spectacle of the event. Others would go through the hoops backward. Each time one of the mermen would do something amazing, the whole audience would cheer them on.

From the far side of the castle at the edge of the pond, the unicorns were waiting with their riders. As the mermen reached the location where the unicorns were waiting, each respective unicorn would take off running in the direction of the town. Their riders held tight to the reins about the unicorn's neck and rode them swiftly through the streets. Everyone in town cheered them on as they passed by them. People along the edge of the roads were screaming and yelling as well as those looking out of the windows of homes and buildings along the race path.

Once the unicorns negotiated their way through the town, they headed across a meadow on the other side toward the line of young dragons waiting. It was only a matter of moments before the unicorns reached them and made contact with their respective dragon.

The first of the dragons took off from the edge of the meadow. Dracon could see the unicorn that he was waiting for fast approaching. As soon as the unicorn made it to him, he leaped from the ground and flew off in the direction of the other dragons. The other dragons had a few seconds' headstarts on him but that didn't matter to him. Merlin felt his heart rising in his throat as he saw that it was now his friend's turn to take part in the race, and hoped that he would do well. Although, part of him already knew that he would.

All the young dragons flew into the thick woods near the meadow. As they entered the woods they turned right and started negotiating their way through the trees following the path of the road leading through them. At one point, they left the road and turned right to follow a stream, which cut through the woods. The stream zigzagged along the woods back and forth.

Occasionally there would be a fallen tree to fly over, and in other places, the branches of the trees were so close to each other stretching across the stream that the dragons had to squeeze through the narrow opening. It would be a combination of speed and agility that would determine who was the leader through this part of the race.

Though Dracon was not as fast as some of the other dragons, his agility was proving to be more than adequate. He had caught up to the rest of the dragons and had taken a slight lead.

It was not long though before the dragons came to the end of the woods and they could see the castle off in the distance. They headed toward the castle where there, in the field near the finish, were laid out many obstacles for them to overcome.

Now that the faster dragons were out of the woods, they began to catch up to Dracon. They then started to retake the lead in the race. However, it was only a matter of moments before they all got to where the obstacles were set up in the field below.

They all began to swoop from side to side, going through the hoops over the field. The audience yelled and screamed in excitement. The young dragons were putting on quite an aerial display for all those watching. It was not that they were showing off. It was just that in order to maneuver through some of the obstacles the dragons had to be quite agile to negotiate them.

They made their final turn around one of the poles at the edge of the field and then raised high into the air to fly over the castle. Dracon, having lost a bit of ground, was now just behind the leaders.

In the field just behind the castle were the racing dragons. Merlin saw the first of the dragons come flying over the roof of the castle but no sign of Dracon. Then a couple of others came over as well. Finally, there was Dracon, hot on the tail of those in the lead.

Merlin was poised and ready. He kept his eye on Dracon and under his breath edged Dracon on. "Come on, Dracon. You can do it," he whispered quietly.

The first of the young dragons reached the racing dragons and each respective one lifted quickly from the ground and began to race for the mountains. Within seconds, Dracon reached the spot where Merlin was and made contact. Merlin's dragon burst from the ground and headed off toward the mountains as well.

Everyone shouted and cheered the riders on, and as soon as the last of the dragons had left the field, almost everyone started finding their way to the front of the castle. The most exciting part of the race would be when the dragons came over the top of the mountain and headed for the finish line.

In the meantime, all of the racing dragons had disappeared into the mist of the mountains in the distance, and the riders were fast approaching the deadly pass into the peaks. Merlin was somewhere at the back of the pack of racers. He realized now that all of the other riders had also held back the day before, as all of the dragons were flying much faster than before. He would have to be especially attentive and exert every bit of concentration he had to run this race.

The first of the riders passed through the gap in the mountains. The others ahead of Merlin also slipped through the opening. Merlin again waited until the last moment to lean forward before allowing the dragon to turn to one side and pass through the gap.

Once on the other side, it was a whole new game. Everyone in the race was now going to be negotiating the mountains along the new path laid out by the royal race master. Merlin could see the other racers just ahead of him. He felt as though he was catching up to them, second-by-second.

The dragons passed the spot where they turned into one of the mountain paths the day before but this time kept going straight, to another opening in the mountains. Then, one by one they began to disappear as they turned.

It wasn't long before Merlin reached the spot and turned as well. He hugged the side of the mountain as close as he could. Every second would count in this race.

At the next turn, there was a ridge they had to go over. Merlin decided he could cut off a few seconds if he had the dragon climb as they approached that turn. He guided the dragon up higher along the wall of the mountain and in seconds they reached the spot where they were to make the turn. When Merlin saw the other dragons, they were still just in front of him but had to make the climb yet to get over the ridge of the mountain ahead of them.

By the time the other riders had gotten high enough to clear the mountain; Merlin had narrowed the gap between them. Being as all of the dragons were evenly matched in speed, it would be the wit and astuteness of the rider that would be the determining factor as to who would win the race. Here early on in this race, Merlin was already proving he was more than capable to take on the more experienced riders. There was still a long way to go in this race yet, and many more obstacles to overcome.

With each turn through the mountains and each ridge and gully to pass through, Merlin was able to find some way of narrowing the lead the others had. They were approaching the canyon of pillars where there would be numerous ways of negotiating this phase of the race.

The riders began to emerge from the treacherous ledges of the mountainside, into a valley where right in front of them were seemingly hundreds of rocky columns, rising up from the canyon floor. They could not fly up over the tops, as that would take too much time, as the next place they were to turn was at the base of the canyon on the other side of all the pillars.

Each rider began negotiating the pillars, in their own style. Because they all wanted to be in position for the turn on the other side, they all chose a different course through the columns so as not to get crowded out by one of the other riders. Too many turns in one direction would cost a rider precious time.

Merlin was negotiating through the columns and was making up for the lost time. This was one of those places on the map, which Merlin had already negotiated in his mind. He was counting the pillars after each turn to determine when to have the dragon turn again. He knew exactly the path he wanted to go through the pillars and was executing the maneuvers perfectly, turning sharply so as not to waste precious time.

When the first of the racers emerged from the pillars, however, it was not Merlin. Within seconds, Merlin and a couple of the other racers appeared from among the pillars not very far behind the lead racer. The first dragon made the turn, and right behind him followed Merlin and the others.

Merlin had narrowed the gap between him and the other riders so much that he was only seconds behind the lead dragon. There was another turn coming up on the right and Merlin got as close as he could to the side. When they got to it, Merlin leaned right and the dragon turned. Just around the curve was a fallen boulder, and the dragon had to stall slightly to fly up over it. The other riders were further out and made it around the huge rock. Merlin had lost seconds and that had cost him a few places in the race.

As the dragons were all making their way through the gorge they had entered, Merlin remembered what Aeem had said to him, "No matter what happens, see yourself crossing the finish line first."

The finish line was swiftly approaching. The racers did not have many more mountain passes to negotiate. The rest of the course was simple, except for the high mountaintop they had to get over which was coming up fast.

Merlin started seeing himself, crossing the finish line just ahead of the other riders. As he had done once before, he had his dragon start climbing higher into the air before reaching the final turn. One of the other racers had started doing the same thing. As had happened before, when they reached the final turn the other dragons were just starting to make their climb toward the top of the mountain, and Merlin again had narrowed their lead slightly.

Nevertheless, they were still ahead of him. He just kept seeing himself crossing the finish line before the other racers. All the dragons continued the climb toward the final peak. The racers began to fly up over the top and were just about to appear on the other side.

All eyes in the kingdom focused on the top of the mountain. The moment of their appearance was already anticipated and there was a hush over the crowd.

As soon as the first dragon appeared, everyone started screaming and cheering. While many people in the kingdom below had a favorite rider or dragon they were rooting for, everyone was cheering simply due to the excitement of the race.

Just as had occurred on the day before, right as the riders appeared over the top of the mountain they started making a beeline right for the finish line. Within seconds of the first dragon's appearance, several other dragons came over the top along with Merlin. All of them except for Merlin took the same beeline toward the finish line.

Merlin had his dragon dive straight down toward the ground below. The dragon pulled in his wings and let gravity take its course. In doing so, the dragon also was able to take a rest from flapping his wings. Merlin and his dragon picked up a great deal of speed with no exertion on the part of the dragon. The other dragons were all using every bit of strength they had trying to get to the finish line first.

When the time was right, Merlin had his dragon pull out of the free fall and begin heading toward the finish line. He was going much faster than the other dragons; however, rather than taking the straight path had taken a more curved path toward the finish, which was just a bit longer than the path the other riders were on. It was yet to be seen whether or not this maneuver on Merlin's part would work.

Everyone watched as all the dragons approached the finish line. It was going to be close.

Merlin's dragon was flying as fast as he could toward the finish line and was still going just a little faster than the other dragons. But as he was leveling off toward the finish line, that speed was dwindling. However, because Merlin had the dragon dip straight down, it might have shaved off those few seconds needed to win the race.

Most everyone below had come to his or her feet now. All eyes focused on the finish line. The royal race master was positioned at the finish line to observe who would be the first to cross.

Dragons were starting to bear down on the finish line at breakneck speed. It was going to be a nose-to-nose finish. As the racers who had taken the straight line were getting close to the finish line, Merlin was fast approaching it just below them.

Everyone was yelling and screaming as loud as they could. In the stands where the Dragon Lord was sitting, everyone stood up as well. Aeem was hoping with all her heart that Merlin would cross the line first. She kept saying to herself that Merlin was going to win.

The moment everyone had waited for had now come. The dragons all began to cross the finish line. It was too close to call who was the winner. Several of the dragons crossed at the same time. It was going to be up to the royal race master to reveal who had won.

Once all the dragons had landed on the field, the royal race master went to the stand where the Dragon Lord was waiting. He approached the Dragon Lord and made the announcement first to the King. Without expression, the

Dragon Lord sat back in his seat waiting for the moment that the royal race master would make the announcement to everyone else in the kingdom.

"The winner of this year's royal race was just by a nose, but a nose just the same. That winner would be Merlin."

There was a roaring sound from the crowd as everyone applauded, and everyone and every creature shouted in admiration of Merlin's accomplishment. Never in all the years of the royal race, has anyone ever won his or her first time participating in the race.

Escorted grandly to the stand where the Dragon Lord awaited, Merlin was about to be hailed as the winner by everyone standing before the platform. When Merlin reached the stage, the royal race master held Merlin's arm up in victory. There was no trophy that would be given out for this accomplishment. However, Merlin's name would be engraved on the wall of winners in the Hall of Fame in the castle. From now and for all time, all who visited the great hall would see Merlin's name.

Aeem was just behind Merlin applauding him. After Merlin indicated his thanks to all before him in the crowd by nodding his head to them, he turned and smiled at Aeem knowing that without her he could not have done it. She was his inspiration and he would be eternally grateful for her help.

The applause from the crowd ended and everyone began to head back to their respective places as well as worlds. It would be another year before the next royal race and they would return again to witness this great event.

Aeem went to Merlin and gave him a hug. As they both stood there smiling at each other, Keltos went over to the two of them.

"It is important that we prepare to leave for your world immediately," he told Merlin. "I will go to your quarters shortly to escort you to the Dragon's Gate and back to your world." He then turned and left to go to the castle.

"I would go to your room with you but the Dragon Lord has something he wants me to do," Aeem told Merlin.

"I can not express to you in words how I feel about what you have done for me and Dracon," Merlin said.

"There is no need. What you have done here today is more than enough. I shall remember our time together forever." She said, holding back the tears. "When I look upon the wall in the Great Hall, I will smile every time I read your name upon it."

"In my mind, I will hold the memory of your face, your voice, and everything about you. Your memory is a gift I will always cherish." Merlin told her.

"Kadil will take Dracon back to your quarters. I am sure you know the way now. I have to go now as the Dragon Lord is expecting me."

Just as Aeem started to turn and walk away, Merlin took her hand. She turned back around and when she did, Merlin took a step toward her, leaned forward, and closing his eyes tightly, he kissed her.

When he opened his eyes, Aeem turned away and walked quickly toward the castle. Merlin watched as she disappeared into the crowd, sadness, and disappointment at having to leave her behind, almost overwhelming him.

There was no huge fanfare, as one would have expected at such an event. Merlin had won, his name would go up on the Royal Wall and those that would come from all corners of the universe would see his name upon it. Everyone who had participated in the race was now part of its history. While the sun would set on this day as it does every day, the memory of what occurred here would live in everyone's memory forever.

Chapter Nineteen

Return to Earth

Merlin was just about ready to leave when there was a knock at the door to his quarters. He walked to the entry to see who the visitor was. It was Keltos. He had come to get Merlin and Dracon for the journey back home. There was no sign of Aeem, Merlin noted with sadness. Merlin had hoped to see her one more time before leaving.

"It is time," Keltos said.

Nodding his head to Keltos, Merlin walked back to the sleeping area. As he looked around one last time, he hoped to himself that someday he might be able to return for another visit. Taking a final glance, he picked up his belongings and headed toward the front door.

Dracon was standing there waiting and could see the disappointed look on Merlin's face.

"Sad. Why?" Dracon asked.

"I'll be all right. I had hoped to see Aeem once more. It is probably better this way." He would never forget her though.

Keltos walked to the door and opened it indicating to Merlin and Dragon that it was time to leave. After Merlin and Dracon passed through the doorway, Keltos closed it behind the three of them; it closed with the sound of finality. He then led Merlin and Dracon back through the castle halls toward the front entry. There was not a soul to be seen anywhere.

Merlin did not expect a big fanfare, as that was not his way. He had just hoped that he would have the opportunity to say goodbye to Aeem.

When they were crossing the bridge that crossed over the pond, Merlin turned and took one last look at the castle. Taking a few brief moments to look about, he then turned and continued to walk toward the Dracon's Gate.

There were people and creatures in the streets celebrating the festivities of the day. Most had already returned to their worlds and in the morning, things would return to normal here on this world as well.

As they approached the Dragon's Gate, Merlin noticed that there was a gathering of people, dragons, and other creatures surrounding the gate. Once Merlin, Dracon, and Keltos got close to the crowd, those who were there moved to one side to let the three of them pass by. One by one, they all made an opening for the three of them to get through. As the three of them passed the outer edge of the crowd, it again closed up and no one could get close to the gate other than those already there.

When they approached the last few people and they stepped aside for the three to pass by, Merlin could see Aeem standing at the gate with the Dragon Lord there by her side.

Merlin was elated to see her. He thought for sure he had seen the last of her earlier on. He would now be able to say his last goodbye though it would not be easy to do.

As soon as Merlin and Dracon got to where the Dragon Lord was standing, a hush came over the crowd. There was silence for what seemed like an eternity. Then, the Dragon Lord broke the silence.

"We have been honored by your visit to our world. When you go back to your world, our thoughts will be with you. You will always be in our hearts and in our minds."

The people in the crowd gave a resounding cheer in support of what the Dragon Lord expressed.

"Because I know how you feel about Aeem and how she feels about you, I have granted her one very special wish. She will be traveling with you to your world to say goodbye. She wanted so much to see your world and I think it is quite fitting that she should be able to escort you back to your world along with Keltos. And after all, she is Dracon's maiden."

Merlin and Aeem looked into each other's eyes. Though this was good news for the two of them, they both knew that the hardest part was yet before them - that of saying goodbye to one another. Yet Merlin was happy that Aeem would get to see his world even if for a brief moment.

Keltos stepped to the center of the gate, with Dracon following him and standing by his side. Merlin took Aeem by the hand and walked her to the center as well. All of them stood there looking around at everyone who had come to wish Merlin farewell. Again, everyone went quiet.

A throng of dragons appeared quite abruptly surrounding the four of them. Then, as fast as they appeared, they disappeared again into the gate.

Merlin watched everything around him begin to vanish just as it had occurred back in his world when he entered the gate to come to this world.

The endless multitude of colors that appeared when Merlin was thrust through space on the journey to the Dragon Lord's world again appeared. This time, it was Aeem that was observing the light show for the first time. The four of them were shooting through space faster than the speed of light. In a matter of moments, the light ceased and darkness surrounded the four of them.

As everything began to appear, Merlin could see that the host of dragons that had come up just before they left the world of the Dragon Lord was surrounding the gate. There was no one else in sight other than the dragons. There were no dragon maidens or pages as before.

Keltos swiftly started to move from the gate and gave instructions to Merlin, Dracon, and Aeem to follow him.

"Come quickly!" He said without hesitation.

The three of them did not question Keltos. They moved as fast as they could to catch up to Keltos and follow his lead. The dragons moved to the side to let the four of them pass by.

Merlin was wondering what was going on. There appeared to be something happening.

Keltos led Merlin, Aeem, and Dracon to a safe place away from the gate.

"Wait here. Whatever you do, do not come near the gate", Keltos instructed them. There was a firmness in his voice that Merlin had not heard before. He would not have dared to disobey the man before, but this seemed to be particularly serious.

Keltos then started to walk back toward the gate and as he did, he began to transform from a man into a dragon. Merlin had not been aware of it; however, Keltos in his true form was actually a pitch black dragon. He was once the head of the royal guard for the Dragon Lord. His assignment was to protect Merlin until such a time as Merlin could fend for himself.

Merlin looked at Aeem in astonishment. Aeem, on the other hand, was not surprised. She had known all along who Keltos was. Merlin realized that he should have known from the moment that he had first laid eyes on the man, from the reaction that Dracon had had when they had first met.

On the other hand, whatever was occurring at the gate was a surprise to both of them. They watched as Keltos and the other dragons waited for what was about to occur, tense and ready, as if they were about to go into battle at any moment.

Without notice, a hoard of beings began to come through the gate in an attempt to gain access to this world. They were humanoid, but shorter, and stouter, with skin that reminded Merlin of that of a toad. They wore only the smallest covering, made of rough leather that seemed to be untreated, and would not have been considered modest in the slightest. In their hands were a variety of weapons, from swords and maces, to longbows, and others that Merlin did not recognize. It was the troll overlords' faithful followers. What they did not know was that the Dragon Lord had sent his best dragons to fend off intruders to this world.

As the troll overlord's followers appeared and immediately rushed forwards, in an obvious attempt to leave the confines of the area. The dragons, of course, did not allow this, and a fierce battle broke out between the trolls and the dragons.

The dragons snapped their teeth at the trolls and used their paws in large, swiping motions. The trolls did not even get close enough to the dragons to be able to use the majority of their weapons, and the worst injuries that they caused were a few split scales on the paws of the dragons. Those with arrows were equally useless, although their lifespans were slightly longer.

While the dragons were distracted by keeping those rushing forwards away, they stood back and fired their arrows, which only glanced harmlessly off the scales of the dragons, and in some cases even pierced the flesh of some of their companions, allowing their sickly green blood to cover the stone floor of the structure. These trolls were soon dead as well, as Keltos breathed in deeply, before opening his mouth, tilting his chin forwards, and releasing a large flame upon them, leaving the terrible smell of burning meat in the air. It was quite apparent that this first wave of trolls was no match for the power of the dragons. They were being defeated with ease.

However, another wave of trolls came through the gate. This time they were much bigger and stronger than the first wave. Not only were there far more of them, but they wore significantly more armor, and they were significantly larger. It was a considerably more fearsome fight with the new band of trolls that appeared in this second wave. The dragons, however, were able to fend them off as well.

With a large crunch, a troll landed next to Merlin. It had been flung up into the air by a dragon that he did not know after it had gotten close enough for the dragon to reach it with its snapping teeth. The full-body, steel plates that it had been wearing served more as a disadvantage than any form of protection. It seemed as if the teeth of the dragon had easily compressed the metal until it had crushed the troll inside, before carelessly throwing it away to deal with the next one. Merlin could clearly see the shape of the dragon's teeth still imprinted over the creature's chest and head.

Not one dragon had fallen victim to the attack by these trolls. But the fight wasn't over yet. As quickly as the dragons defeated the second wave, another wave of assailants appeared at the gate and began to attempt their entrance into this world.

This time there were other creatures mixed in with the trolls. The troll overlord had acquired help from other creatures from worlds analogous to his own. They were mole-like, Merlin decided, or at least that was the best comparison that he could draw. They seemed to be completely blind and moved around using their wriggling noses. They had large, formidable claws that worked far better than the pathetic weapons of the troll overlord, and could easily slice through the scales of the dragons, causing their bright red blood to flow freely for the first time in the battle. It was clear that the troll overlord was intent on gaining access to this world and was ready to battle whatever force may attempt to keep him from his objective.

As the dragons were fighting off this new wave of creatures and trolls, the troll overload himself appeared through the gate and joined the battle. The mêlée was now in full force. Because of the fierceness of this last band of attackers, some of the dragons were now falling victim to them.

Merlin could not help but gasp as he felt tears rising in his eyes. Occasionally, a flash of light would appear, before the dragon seemed to disappear into nothingness, leaving behind only a beautiful gemstone. Their physical bodies were dying.

The dragons were, up to this point, able to keep any of the intruders from leaving the immediate area of the gate. Though now and then one would get past the confines of the gate, they didn't go far before being cast down by one of the dragons.

Merlin, Aeem, and Dracon watched seemingly helplessly from a short distance away. What could they do against such formidable odds? Such creatures entering the gate would kill them immediately.

The numbers of dragons were dwindling and yet more attackers were coming through the gate. There didn't seem to be an end to the onslaught. It was becoming apparent that the troll overlord would be successful in gaining entrance into Merlin's world.

There was only one way to stop the attack. Merlin was the only one who was free to take the action necessary to end this. All the dragons were busy fighting off the attackers.

Merlin realized it was up to him to bring the battle to an end. He remembered what the Dragon Lord told him about the Spirita Stone. It had the power to create and the power to destroy. Merlin would have to destroy the gate so that no more creatures could come to this world.

He stood up from behind the rock he and Aeem were hiding behind. Then he raised his arm up high with the staff in hand. He closed his eyes and saw the gate, as it was when he first came to this place. The Spirita Stone at the end of his staff began to light up. The stone got brighter and brighter. Merlin opened his eyes. He then held the staff out toward the gate and a blinding beam of light shot out from the blazing Spirita Stone.

An explosive sound came from the direction of the gate and a cloud of smoke and dust immediately encompassed it. As the cloud began to clear, Merlin could see the dragons fighting the last of the troll overlord's horde. Now that there were no more attackers coming through the gate the dragons began killing off what was left of the attackers.

Keltos moved toward the troll overlord to take him on himself. Though the troll overlord was very large in stature and had weapons he was using against the dragons, this did not sway Keltos. There was only one dragon that had the ability to defeat the overlord. And it was only fitting that this dragon was Keltos himself.

The last of the overlord's mob fell to the earth. Keltos was ready to fight the overlord. The overlord was wrought with anger and would not stop fighting. Though his demise was imminent, he was not going to relent.

The dragons backed away to allow these last two to do battle on their own.

The overlord charged Keltos. He swung his weapon at him but Keltos dodged the attack. Keltos breathed fire at the overlord but the overlord blocked the flames with his shield.

The two of them continued to wrangle, taking turns attacking and each fending off the other attack. One of the others would make a fatal mistake eventually that would allow the other to claim victory. But it was not to occur quickly. The overlord was well conditioned to do battle. Both he and Keltos were seasoned fighters. The battle raged on.

Then the opening needed to strike a lethal blow presented itself. Keltos fell back to the ground and the overlord took a strike at Keltos with his weapon. He was so sure that he was about to strike Keltos with a killing blow that he put all his might into it. This was exactly what Keltos wanted the overlord to do. Just as the overlord made his final approach and was in the last stage of his swing with his weapon, Keltos sprung up from the ground vaulting over the head of the overlord. It was too late for the overlord. He could not stop his assault.

Keltos struck the overlord from behind striking a blow to the head. The overlord fell briefly to the ground. He lost hold of his shield. He got back to his feet but now only had his weapon to defend himself. This is not enough against a dragon's fire. He was now totally vulnerable. Yet still, he would not relent.

He moved once again to attack Keltos. A stream of fire came from Keltos and enveloped the overlord. Badly burned but nonetheless determined, the overlord took another swing at Keltos. Keltos rose from the ground into the air this time using his broad tail to strike the overlord. The overlord fell to the ground once more. This time he did not get up as quickly as he had done before. He did however rise to his feet one last time.

Keltos could only show mercy to the overlord and end his torment quickly. He transformed back into a man. He went over to where one of the overlord's minion's weapons lay and picked it up. The overlord was very weak however; he attempted to strike Keltos again. Using the weapon, Keltos struck the final blow that finished him. The overlord dropped to the ground. It was not but a few moments later that he took his final breath.

Though many had fallen dead this day around Dragon's Gate, there were barely any bodies to be found. The dragons that had all passed on had left gemstones in their place and most of the troll overlord's followers were burned up in the flames of the dragons or disintegrated from the blast that destroyed Dragons Gate.

Now that the battle had ended, Elfins began to appear to collect the gemstones to take them to their proper resting place. All signs that this battle had taken place would soon be gone.

Merlin, Aeem, and Dracon came out from where they were and went to where the remaining dragons and Keltos were standing.

"You did as was expected of you, Merlin," Keltos said.

"The Dragon Lord knew that this was going to happen?" Merlin asked.

"He had been sensing for days that the overlord had sent spies to his world. There were those keeping a close eye on them. They were heard talking about the plan to attack your world."

"But now Aeem can not get back." Merlin asserted.

"He did not plan for her to return. She has always been free to go where she chooses. She chose to come with you to your world, and thus that is where she will stay."

Keltos held out his hand as if pointing to something.

In the forest where the Tome was sitting upon the stump, the bright light began to pour out from it. The cover of the Tome opened and a burst of air and light came pouring out from within the book.

Merlin, Dracon, Aeem, and Keltos all four came out from the Tome and appeared standing next to the stump surrounding it. Merlin was now back in his world in his own time period again, along with Keltos and Dracon and his special friend Aeem.

Chapter Twenty

Slightly Off Course

The shadow of something could be seen moving through the grass and when Merlin looked up to see what it was, Paradream came gliding down from overhead and landed close by. He walked over to where Merlin and the others were standing.

"I trust you had an enjoyable and enlightening experience," Paradream said.

"Very much so," Merlin replied.

"And you have brought someone back with you," Paradream said.

"This is Aeem."

"It is very nice to meet you Aeem."

"Likewise," she replied with a slight bow.

Looking at Merlin, Paradream said, "You will have to tell me about your venture into the Tome sometime. I would like to hear all about it."

"That I will do, when we have a whole lot of time to kill, I promise," Merlin said.

Then eyeing Dracon, Paradream stated,

"Dracon. I sense that there is something different about you."

"Yes. Different." Dracon replied.

"Oh. I see. You are speaking. This will certainly make life more interesting." Paradream said jokingly.

"Keltos, my old friend, it appears that we have our work cut out for us now. Merlin's journey is just beginning and there is so much yet to be done to prepare him for his destiny."

"I agree. However, it is a future I am sure he will be prepared for and face with great strength and fortitude." Keltos said firmly.

"I agree," Paradream replied.

"We have a bit of a journey ahead of us and I am sure that Merlin would like to be on his way, don't you think," Paradream said to Keltos while looking at Merlin.

"Yes. You know the way." Keltos replied to Paradream. "I will be seeing you again soon," Keltos said to Merlin.

"You are not coming with us?" Merlin asked.

"Not right now. I have some things I need to take care of first." Keltos informed Merlin.

Keltos then turned to Aeem and said, "You are in good company. I am sure you are already aware of this. Keep an eye on him. While I am away, you are his anamchara. However, don't let that get in the way of anything else that may develop between you. A person can be an anamchara and a close companion too. I am sure you know what I mean."

Aeem gave him a timid smile. Not that she was the kind of person to be shy by any means, however, the only one she had ever heard speak to her like a father figure was the Dragon Lord himself.

Keltos took Aeem's hand and led her over to Paradream. He then lifted her onto the stallion's back.

Pointing to the Tome, Keltos said, "You might want to bring that along."

Merlin went over to the stump and took the Tome in his arm, then he moved over to where Keltos stood and Keltos helped Merlin up, placing him just behind Aeem.

He then stepped back from Paradream and transformed back to his form as a dragon. Looking over at Dracon he said, "You be safe my brother. Take good care of Merlin. He will take good care of you." He then looked over toward Aeem and said with a smile, "Moreover, enjoy the fact that you now have a maiden to tend to you as well."

Dracon looked over toward Aeem and raised his brow. He realized Merlin had not only gained a friend, moreover, but he had also retained this new companion too.

"Aeem. Maiden. Sing."

When Dracon looked back toward Keltos, Keltos had spread his huge wings out and now thrust them against the wind lifting from the ground. He then disappeared over the treetops, leaving laughter echoing behind him.

Once Keltos was out of sight, Paradream flapped his wings briskly and lifted into the air. He then began to move swiftly forward, flying up over the trees. Dracon followed close behind.

Aeem was astonished at how pretty the Earth was. It was everything Merlin had described to her.

Paradream would often fly low so that Aeem could get a close look at the beautiful streams and waterfalls along the way. He would then lift high into the sky now and again so that she could also see far off into the horizon.

Some of the sights along the way looked familiar to Merlin. He remembered some of the things he had seen when Paradream first took him to the forest where he had entered the Tome.

Dracon flew up close to Paradream and did a spin or two showing off his agility and aerial skills. Aeem held her arms out wide pretending she was flying as well. Merlin held out one of his arms as well as he didn't want to let go of the Tome he was holding with the other.

They were all having the time of their lives.

Merlin began to recognize some of the places they flew over and that they were getting closer to the cove. He knew they would be there soon.

However, Paradream instead took a turn South heading away from the cove. Merlin wondered what

Paradream was doing. Why was he going away from the cove?

Paradream lifted high into the sky so that Merlin and Aeem could see the ocean off in the distance. The sun was almost touching the horizon. It was a beautiful sunset in the making.

After traveling down the coast not too far from where the cove was, Paradream began his descent. The lower he dropped the further the sun got to the line of the horizon. They were so high up that they could tell that darkness was already falling on the land to the East of the mountains below.

Going around one of the peaks of the mountains, Paradream began a straight path toward a small valley on the western slope of one of the hills.

Merlin pointed to the valley showing Aeem where there were people moving about. They were still too far off to see who they could be.

As they got closer some of the people on the ground started shouting to the others that a dragon was approaching. Those that were indoors, came out to see what the ruckus was all about.

Out of one of the doors stepped a couple of figures that Merlin was well acquainted with. It was his mother and father. Anabe put her hands to her mouth. She could not tell who the two people on the back of Paradream were, however, she had a good idea who one of them was.

Merlin had already recognized his parents on the ground below. He was anxious for Paradream to land so he could go give his mother a hug and a hearty handshake to his dad.

Everyone began running to an open field where they knew Paradream could land safely. No one was running faster than Anabe and her husband. As fast as their feet could take them, they hurried to the field.

Paradream was just gliding down from the sky ready to touch the ground. Anabe did not even wait for his hooves to touch the earth. She took off to where Paradream was touching down following close to his wing as he pulled them back.

Aeem raised her right leg over to the side with her left leg and slid off Paradream. Merlin did likewise and as soon as his feet touched the ground; his mother took him in her arms. There wasn't a dry eye to be found among anyone. Everyone that had lived with Anabe over the last year or so knew of her anguish and all had hoped that Merlin would return to the village one day safely. The day everyone prayed for had just arrived.

Merlin's father too joined in along with Anabe in giving his son a welcome home hug. He missed his son a great deal, and was relieved at his return. As the three of them were embracing, Aeem along with everyone else was happily watching them. It was a reunion whose time had come.

After a short while, Anabe finally released her hold on Merlin and turned her attention to the new arrival. Wondering who the person could be, she looked over at Merlin and asked, "Who is this?"

"This is Aeem," Merlin replied.

"Aeem, I am glad to meet you," Anabe said.

"You'll have to tell me all about yourself."

Anabe took Aeem by the hand then reached over and took Merlin's as well. The two of you have arrived just in time for dinner. I had not planned on four people; however, it will only take a few minutes to prepare enough for everyone."

She began to lead Merlin and Aeem toward their cabin among the trees just up the hillside. As soon as the three of them began to head up the hillside, everyone left to return to their respective cabins.

"Paradream, thanks for getting Merlin back safely," Myrd said gratefully.

"I had little to do with that," Paradream replied. "I am sure that Merlin has some interesting stories to share with you."

"I look forward to hearing every one of them too."

"Until the time comes for us to see each other again." Paradream said to Myrd.

He then lifted from the ground and flew off toward the ocean's shore then turned to the North.

Myrd watched until Paradream was no longer in sight. Then he turned in the direction of his cabin in the woods to see Anabe leading Merlin and Aeem toward their home just inside the line of trees up the hill.

Looking at Dracon, Myrd said, "It's good to have you home too. You better come with me; I have a place prepared just for you."

The two of them began walking up the hillside in the direction of the others. Merlin and his family were finally reunited. The stories of what had occurred over the last year were yet to be shared and their futures were yet to unfold.

Made in the USA
Columbia, SC
15 April 2022

58694104R00109